CONTEMPORARY URDU SHORT STORIES FROM KOLKATA

Translated by **Shams Afif Siddiqi**

Edited by **Shams Afif Siddiqi** & **Fuzail Asar Siddiqi**

THORNBIRD
NIYOGI BOOKS

Published by
NIYOGI BOOKS
Block D, Building No. 77,
Okhla Industrial Area, Phase-I,
New Delhi-110 020, INDIA
Tel: 011-26818960, +91 7428978881
Email: niyogibooks@gmail.com
Website: www.niyogibooksindia.com

Editor: Shaurya Shaukat Sircar
Design: Nadeem Ahmed
Cover Design: Misha Oberoi

ISBN: 978-93-89136-90-6
Publication: 2023

Price: ₹495

Printed at: Niyogi Offset Pvt. Ltd., New Delhi, India

Fakhruddin Siddiqi 'Asar'
Former Reader of Urdu,
Maulana Azad College, Calcutta

Contents

PREFACE

For a long time, Urdu short stories have been translated into English. Some important names had initiated the work of translation. They translated writers from India as well as Pakistan. In the beginning, old and classical writers were taken up. Recently, even individual writers were translated with favourable reviews. An anthology came out with pan-Indian short story writers finding space. But one thing was sadly missing. Except for one or two, writers from West Bengal, especially Kolkata, did not find representation. So, one afternoon, while walking around in the campus of Jawaharlal Nehru University, when my eldest son Huzaifa Omair Siddiqi suddenly put a question to me, I stood still, as if someone had shaken up my soul: 'Why don't you translate Urdu short story writers from Kolkata and give them a different readership?' When I blinked, he went on: 'You know both Urdu and English languages well.' I thought for a while, but the idea stuck in the recesses of my mind.

Back home in Kolkata, I called up some old friends. I asked them to bring anthologies/works of writers who were either born in the city or lived and wrote here. I do not know whether that was the right thing to do. I had no intention of belittling others who were not from the city. I just wanted to put Urdu writers from Kolkata before the English-reading public, who must have been eager to know what they had been doing all these years. They must have been curious about their subject matter, treatment, and how they were similar and yet different from other writers in India and Pakistan. After all, Kolkata had always been a hub of literary activities since the British era.

The number of works threw up a challenge. I came up with a theme, thinking that it could ease my problem of selection. To some extent, it did. The other parameter was the story's readability. There were dozens of stories that were normal in the Urdu language but would have appeared out of place for a non-Urdu reader. At no point do I claim to be an expert. I also feel that I might not have done justice to those not included in my list. My selection does not prove that those left out were not good writers or, that their stories were not worth reading. It was incidental that they did not fit my list. I had to start somewhere and so with stumbling steps, I began. I do not know whether nature scorned at my efforts. For soon, one of the worst calamities of this century threw cold water on my efforts. Covid-19 made its appearance, and what the country and the world witnessed had now become a dark chapter in history. In a different way, it also proved to be a boon. With lockdowns and life coming to a standstill, I was stuck in the corner of my room. I read as many stories as possible. I did the preliminary selection and straightaway started the work of translation. Initially, I translated only nine stories. But as time went on and my confidence grew, I went on adding till I reached this number.

A word about my translation: I do not want to go into the intricacies of the term, but I tried to stick to the original as far as possible without making it appear strange in a language like English. The problem had increased with Urdu writers nowadays writing from a totally different perspective, thereby making it difficult to transfer the idea to another language without getting caught in a dilemma of sorts. For example, Firoz Abid sometimes uses abstract words and expressions. The language may not look out of place in Urdu, but if translated faithfully, the English rendering would not only look strange, it would be un-English. Mahmoud Yasien's stories hover around dreams. He uses punctuation and clichés that create hurdles in the translation. But once rendered, the stories look perfectly normal, as if the writer had thought and written them in the English language itself. Whether his stories found due place or not is not known. His translated ones will be liked because of their strange thought and settings. Similarly, Anis

Rafi's 'The Inner Fort' was written in ornate Urdu, almost the kind that was used in the 19th century. It was a challenge for me, as also the length, which was closer to that of a novella. The readers may find it time-consuming, but I think it would be worth reading this story. These writers do not only violate some basic tenets of the genre; they sometimes improve and even transcend the boundaries.

All the writers have established their names in one way or the other. If the readers like the stories, it will be because of the writers' work. If they do not, there must be something wrong with my translation. I have tried my best to keep inconsistencies at bay. If they do occur, consider them to be my shortcomings. If it is smooth reading, give credit to my co-editor and the editorial team at Niyogi Books. They have worked days on end to make the manuscript readable.

At the outset, I must thank Niyogi Books for accepting the book for publication. I also want to thank Dr Nirmal Kanti Bhattacharjee for reading the initial submission, considering my translation fit for publication and bearing with the delays of the final manuscript. Thanks are due to Ms Tultul Niyogi for signing the agreement and looking at the intricacies of official works. I would be doing an injustice to Ms Bishnupriya Chowdhuri, Editor of *The Antonym*, if I do not remember her contribution. Apart from them, there are so many people who have, in one way or the other, helped in the process of reading/

writing and editing, that it is not possible to name them individually. I thank all these wonderful people who came along and stayed with me till the end. Lastly, I must thank my wife, Syeda Afshan, for bearing with me for the last three years while I worked on the book. Never for a moment did she complain when I shirked domestic responsibilities and turned the house into a litter of books, papers, notes, etc.

I hope the book proves to be popular with the readers. It would inspire me for future efforts.

Shams Afif Siddiqi

INTRODUCTION

The short story, as opposed to the novel, had a difficult time trying to establish itself as a respectable genre. Though for more than a century it had made its presence felt in Western literature, it was denied serious critical attention in proportion to its importance.[1] It was only when the term 'short story' was entered in the supplement to the Oxford English Dictionary (OED) in 1933[2] that the genre eventually gained its due recognition in the literary world. One of the reasons for this can be its flexibility to cater to the demands of 19th-century readership. The other was, perhaps, its inability to express the range of human experience, its depth and complexity, the shade within shades of emotions that were successfully portrayed in novels. But slowly, the genre managed to secure a place. The best of writers could not afford to avoid it; practitioners used it with experimental ease, and discerning readers and publishers started taking an interest.

1 Ian Reid, *The Short Story* (London and New York: Metheun, 1977), 1.

2 Ibid., 1.

It is difficult to trace its history; some examples are cited from Old and New Testaments, which contained stories and parables. But they were didactic and devoid of literary features. Ancient Egypt had innumerable stories like the *Shipwrecked Sailor* written around the second millennium BC that entertained readers. There were Greek and Roman tales of Petronius' *Satyricon* and Apuleius' *Metamorphoses* in the first and second century AD.[3] Similarly, there were Greek and Latin verse narratives in the first century AD, but the 'Milesian' tales of Aristides of Miletus (c. 100 BC) translated into Latin[4] caught attention because of their human touches. The best example is the story of the *Widow of Ephesus* related by Petronius.[5] The power of this story can be understood by the manner in which it had been retold in the 12th, 17th, and even the 20th centuries by writers like John of Salisbury, La Fontaine, and Christopher Fry.[6] Apart from these, there was traditional storytelling that included centuries of oriental tales like the *Panchatantra* and the *One Thousand and One Nights*. In Europe, it was Boccaccio's *Decameron* that had enormous influence on the Renaissance narrative. It is interesting to know that in France, magazines

3 Ibid., 16.

4 Ibid., 16.

5 Ibid., 17.

6 Ibid., 18.

had started publishing *contes*, stories of Merimee, Balzac, and Gautier around 1829–31. They were followed by Daudet's *Lettres de Mon Moulin* (1869), Flaubert's Trois Contes (1877) and Maupassant's stories in the 1880s.[7] In Russia, Pushkin's *Tales of Bjelkin* (1830) made an impact because the narrative became the focus of attention. Gogol and Turgenev managed to improve the short fiction's form and content. 'The Overcoat' of Gogol became so important for Russian literature that Turgenev went to the extent of saying: 'We have all come out from under Gogol's Overcoat'.[8]

Short stories in America became popular in the 19th century. Regular magazines published them with an eye to readers for a quick read. The American periodicals and magazines made it popular and shaped its forms. The trivial romance and Gothic tales were soon replaced by stories of writers like Washington Irving and Edgar Allan Poe who improved the form through their subject matter and treatment. But they were still away from what technically could be called a 'short story'. Irving called his works 'sketches' or 'short tales'.[9] Poe believed that the American periodicals, with their emphasis on brevity could be the congenial way forward for

7 Ibid., 24.

8 Ibid., 24.

9 Martin Scofield, ed., *The Cambridge Introduction to the American Short Story* (Cambridge and New York: Cambridge University Press, 2006), 6.

American literature as a whole,[10] and the form also provided writers a platform and a paycheck. This contributed most to the development of the short stories. Writers started writing stories in form and content that the magazine publishers were interested in buying. The focus of short stories on one or two characters made Frank O'Connor link it with the idea of romanticism, of lonely, isolated characters.[11]

An interesting feature down the centuries is the genre's changing variety, making it difficult to be classified under any fixed notion. It is strange that even today, not much theoretical work has been undertaken except by the writers themselves. Unlike the English, the Russians and the French had taken up formalist criticism of the genre.[12] The necessity of plot in the 19th century underwent a transformation with the arrival of modern writers. Even the concept of characterisation and narration took a beating with the postmodern writers. But still, some basic features remained in order that it may be called a 'story'. The oft-quoted line of E.M. Forster about the novel: 'Yes—oh dear yes—the novel tells a story'[13] can also be said about the short story. Whatever may be the subject matter, structure, or style, a short story tells a 'story';

10 Ibid., 7.

11 Ibid., 8.

12 Ian Reid, *The Short Story* (London and New York: Metheun, 1977), 3.

13 E.M. Forster, *Aspects of the Novel* (New York: Rosetta Books, 2002), 21.

otherwise, readers would not read it. Again, the question of what constitutes a 'story' has been discussed extensively by theorists. Whether events, in their stages of development or sequential movements and logical relationship, are enough for it to be considered a story have been debated so often that it is not necessary to repeat them here. What neither theorists nor writers forget is Aristotle's advice, about the plot, in his *Poetics*, that it must have a beginning, middle, and end.[14] In a novel as well as in a short story, a plot is necessary, though a sea change has occurred in the second half of the 20th century with writers experimenting in diverse ways. Today, fiction can be disjunctive,[15] like weird dreams, or include theories that defy definitions. Franz Kafka's 'A Country Doctor' does not follow the usual sequential plot. Yet it had moved generations to unravel its plot or grasp the surrealistic meaning that eludes while it mystifies. Jorge Luis Borges' 'The Garden of Forking Paths' challenges the usual distinction that exists between cause, effects, and the narrative medium. Stories like these appeal to the intellect of the reader. It forces them to make sense of disjointed ideas or narratives. Ian Reid called them 'anti-stories',[16] yet they must be seen as part of the whole and should not be judged in isolation.

---

14 Ian Reid, *The Short Story* (London and New York: Metheun, 1977), 6.

15 Ibid., 7.

16 Ibid., 8.

Much has also been written about the length of a short story. One need not go into detail as it is beyond the scope of the work. We can only say that some stories are as short as comprising a few pages; others run into 30 or 40 pages. If the reader is able to read the complete story in a single sitting, that can be said to be its ideal length. Much has been written and discussed about the difference that exists between a novel and a short story. Again, this is not the appropriate place to initiate a discussion about the two important genres. As far as the short story is concerned, readers have opted for it because of the beauty that lies within its compact structure, a beauty that thrills the reader when the story ends.

The history of the Urdu short story is remarkably different from its Western counterpart. Unlike in the West, the Urdu story had its germination with the *dastan* or the tale that was popular from ancient times, dealing with kings and princes amidst supernatural surroundings. They were passed on through the generations orally and entertained adults and children alike. There is *Alif Laila* that still entertains people. The *dastan*s had the element of romance that evaporated with the arrival of reason and worries about social issues. Though 19th-century publications like Mir Amman's *Baagh-o-Bahar* (1801), Rajab Ali Beg Suroor's *Fasaana-e-Ajaa'ib* (1834), and Pandit Ratan Nath Sarshar's

Fasaana-e-Azaad broke new grounds, they still carried on the tradition of the *dastan*.

The *dastan* brings to the fore the different possibilities of man's self. It marks the collision of nature with man's ego.[17] But all that came to an end with the defeat of Dara Shikoh, the failure of the First War of Independence of 1857 and the Aligarh movement. Sir Syed Ahmed Khan's writings drove out the poetic element that had been a part of respectable prose.[18] Nazir Ahmed (1830–1912) tried to put a break to this tradition with his novels of morals. Abdul Halim Sharar (1860–1926) resorted back to elements of the *dastan*, thereby indicating its importance in the mind of the readers. Mirza Muhammad Hadi Ruswa's *Umrao Jan Ada* (1899), the first Urdu novel in the true sense of the term, made the ground congenial for fiction in Urdu. It was during this time that Urdu short story writing was also making its appearance.

The interesting part was that the first Urdu story writers did not totally do away with this important tradition. Rashidul Khairi, Sultan Hyder Josh, Sajjad Hyder Yildirim, Neyaz Fatehpuri, and even Premchand, to some extent, made use of the *dastan*.[19] Though the first short story writers started their journey under its influence, the fast-changing political and

17 Dr Mirza Hamid Beg, *Urdu Afsane Ki Rawayet 1903–1990* (Islamabad: Academy Adibiyat Pakistan, Islamabad, 1991), 28.

18 Ibid., 28.

19 Ibid, 29.

social life made them adopt ways that removed them from the roots.

Though Munshi Premchand (1880–1936) is considered to be the first significant Urdu short story writer in the true sense, according to Dr Mirza Hamid Beg, the first Urdu short story writer was Rashidul Khairi. His book *Urdu Afsane ki Rawayet* (1903–1990) published by Academy Adibiyat Pakistan, Islamabad, in 1991, is dedicated: 'To the first Urdu short story writer Rashidul Khairi'. Ali Jawad Zaidi though claims that it was Sajjad Hyder Yildirim who wrote the first story in 1900 titled 'Nashe ki Pehli Tarang', a few years before Premchand's first story 'Duniya Ka Sabse Anmol Ratan'.[20] Intizar Hussain, on the other hand, thought that the decline of the Urdu short story had started with Premchand.[21]

Rashidul Khairi (1868–1936) took the responsibility to rectify society in his stories. He also took up the rights of women. He was against the foreign domination of India. His story 'Siyah Daagh' dealt with the Jallianwala Bagh massacre and showed his patriotism and dream of India's Independence. Sultan Hyder Josh also wrote patriotic stories and was against foreign domination. The list of Urdu writers who contributed to the history of the short story is not insignificant, though

20 Ali Jawad Zaidi, *A History of Urdu Literature* (Delhi: Sahitya Akademi, 1993), 391.

21 Dr Mirza Hamid Beg, *Urdu Afsane Ki Rawayet 1903–1990* (Islamabad: Academy Adibiyat Pakistan, Islamabad, 1991), 19.

most have been forgotten. Hamidullah Afsar focused on the neglected sections of Muslim society and had command over the craft of fiction. Ali Abbas Hussaini had a love for romance and a natural flair for the portrayal of characters. Akhtar Orainvi portrayed village life in Bihar but also wrote about men and women of towns from the lower strata of society. Azam Karevi was known for his character portrayal. He placed characters in different situations and studied them psychologically. Jalil Kidwai's first story came out in 1919. He is known more as a translator, but his own stories had deeper implications. His language depicts the chaste idiom of Delhi. Md Mujib, on the other hand, is known as the translator of Russian stories, especially Chekhov, but his collection of 1932 brought him into prominence in the history of Urdu story writing. Upender Nath Ashk, like Premchand, wrote in Urdu and Hindi and was a prolific writer. Hayatullah Ansari wrote on various subjects and had a grasp over technique and language. Akhtar Ansari Dehlavi's stories were full of passionate subjects. 'Asli Badnaseeb' is the story of a loser who suddenly wins a lottery, but that turns out to be his worst failure. Sohail Azimabadi wrote about Bihar's towns and villages and portrayed the injustices of social life.

Majnu Gorakhpuri started a new trend which was a mix of romance and philosophy. He was influenced by Hegel and the English novelist Thomas Hardy. He introduced such romances in his collection *Siman Posh* that made the youths crazy.[22] Mrs Abdul Qadir's first collection *Lashoon Ka Shahar Aur Doosre Afsane* was published in 1916. She was appreciated because of her portrayal of the supernatural and was influenced by Edgar Allen Poe.[23] Another lady who created ripples was Hijab Imtiaz Ali whose stories move around mystery and romance and unforgettable characters. Her depiction of the nature of South India became a part of the landscape of her stories.[24]

Mirza Adeeb's collections like *Sehra Naward Ke Khutoot* and *Sehra Naward Ke Roman* were his attempts to come out of the basic attributes of *dastan*, a struggle between his love of romance and zest for realism. In 1932, Prof Md. Mujib's collection of stories, *Kimiyagar*, paved the way for a new path for Urdu short stories. *Angare*, a collection of nine stories and a play, published in the same year, added life to it. *Angare* had five stories of Sajjad Zaheer, one story and one play by Rashid Jahan, two stories by Ahmed Ali, and one story by Mahmuduzzafar. Apart from the influence of Marx, the collection had pan-European influences. Ironically, *Angare*, which means 'embers', was taken out of stalls in the different parts of the country and consigned to flames by the public. They considered it to be an

22 Ibid., 57.

23 Ibid., 57–58.

24 Ibid., 60–61.

attack on eastern thoughts. *Angare* was an attempt to introduce modernist tendencies in Urdu literature by importing the techniques of the stream of consciousness of writers like James Joyce into Urdu fiction, although in a rudimentary form, especially in the stories of Sajjad Zaheer and Ahmed Ali. The *Angare* quartet's attempt was to introduce important questions about sexuality, freedom of speech, and women's issues into the public consciousness.

It is said that Sajjad Zaheer and Ahmed Ali drew the initial draft of the *Anjuman Taraqqi Pasand Musannifeen* (Progressive Writers' Association) in one of the corners of Lucknow University Library in 1932.[25] It was finally declared in 1933 by Ahmed Ali, Mahmuduzzafar, and Rashid Jahan with Sajjad Zaheer sending his letter of approval from London. Initially, the aim was literary, and the only political part was taking up problems of life, especially of people from the subcontinent. But from the beginning, the Progressive Writers' Association stressed upon ideas that blocked avenues for future writers. The movement produced some great names; amongst them were Mulk Raj Anand, Devender Satyarthi, Khwaja Ahmed Abbas, Akhtar Hussain Raipuri, Krishan Chandar, Aziz Ahmed, Ismat Chughtai, Rajinder Singh Bedi, Ahmed Nadim Qasmi, Balwant Singh, and so on.

---

25 Ibid., 67. Refers to an Interview of Ahmed Ali by Saher Ansari, 1969–70, Karachi.

Angare had set a new trend which was supplemented by the publication of Ahmed Ali's collection *Sholay* in 1934. Psychological interrogation and sensationalism became the norm, and writers ranging from Saadat Hasan Manto to Wajida Tabassum indulged freely in it. The influence of Freud and European fiction played an important part. Manto, Md Hasan Askari, Mumtaz Mufti, Syed Fayyaz Mahmood, Agha Babar, Abul Fazal Siddiqui, Khan Fazlur Rahman and Syed Rafique Hussain are some of the important names.

Another turn took place in Urdu short story writings after 1947. Apart from writing about the human displacement on both sides of the border, writers sketched individual pictures of human tragedy. Manto, Krishan Chandar, Intizar Husain, Quarratulain Hyder, Ashfaque Ahmed, Md Khalid Akhtar, Kartar Singh Duggal, Bano Qudsia and others tried to make sense of the chaos of the new world order. Modernism and postmodernism changed the way Western writers looked at art and literature. Urdu fiction, and more so, the short story, was also deeply affected by them. It could be a reaction to the excesses of the Progressive movement or other socio-political changes, but around the 1960s and 1970s, writers put aside their political affiliations and wrote about the lonely individual with a new formula of structure and imagery. Literary journals in India and Pakistan published their stories, and for more than 20 years, the craze held the public in awe. Writers like Surender

Prakash, Anwar Sajjad, Joginder Paul, Khalida Hussain, Balraj Komal, Ghias Ahmed Gaddi, Md Mansha Yaad, Mirza Hamid Beg and Shamsur Rahman Faruqi managed to keep the trend alive.[26]

The modernist Urdu short story shifted away from the earlier emphasis of the Progressive Writers who were writing about social issues to a renewed focus on probing the interiority of the human psyche. Both Shamsur Rahman Faruqi and Muhammad Umar Memon give credit to some extent to Manto's 1955 short story 'Phunde' as attempting to bring about this turn away from social reality to an engagement with the chaotic and unpredictability of human consciousness.[27] Even in the case of later writers such as Anwar Sajjad, Surender Prakash and the like, there was no one style which prevailed; some introduced the strange and the uncanny through realistic depictions of everyday life, while others tampered with the form of the short story itself to eke out the strangeness of human existence. The short story after the 1960s became synonymous with a symbolic mode of expression in an attempt to articulate the fragmentary nature of modern existence. Here too, Naiyer Masud introduced a new trend in his short stories, which were

26 Ibid., 67–99.

27 Shamsur Rahman Faruqi, "Modern Urdu Literature", In *Modern Indian Literature: An Anthology. Vol 1: Surveys and Poems*, ed. by K.M. George (New Delhi: Sahitya Akademi, 1992), 420–445; Muhammad Umar Memon, "Urdu Short Story: The Modernist Phase (1950s and After)", *Dawn*, May 25, 2014, https://www.dawn.com/news/1108350.

published as a collection from the 1980s onwards. His stories seem strange and out of this world, yet remain integrated to the human psyche. The stories are different but strangely related to each other by a sensibility of art and psychology. Probably he was trying to delve deeper into man's self to find out meaning that somehow remains suspended somewhere. Masud's stories require a more sympathetic understanding and critical analysis to arrive at a meaning.

Calcutta, now Kolkata, had always been the hub of writers, Bengali or Urdu. Bankim Chandra Chattopadhyay, the great Bengali novelist and Rabindranath Tagore, one who wrote in diverse genres, were from this city. The history of Urdu in Bengal is interesting, as also the contributions of Wajid Ali Shah and the establishment of Fort William College. From the beginning, the progress of Urdu prose, down to modern times, is replete with achievements that require serious studies. Calcutta was also the centre for poets who nurtured the muse even in the 1960s but somehow were not given prominence because of regional prejudice. But short story writers from Kolkata made a name for themselves in India and Pakistan.

This book is a modest compilation of writers, all of them living, except one, to showcase their capacity to handle this important genre with ease and spontaneity. The story writers have exploited its different facets with seriousness and sometimes with humour. The eight writers have been selected with an eye to the readability of their stories. The 19 stories, on the other hand, have one thing in common, and that is the idea of a 'quest' that lies somewhere in between. Every story is in search of the unattainable—sometimes unfathomable as in Mahmoud Yasien's stories or the abstract as in Firoz Abid's; in others, they are closer to reality, and yet remain beyond the reach of the characters.

Sayeed Premi is the only writer included in the collection who is not alive today. 'The Dawn of Realisation' is the story of a young girl who was rejected by her would-be in-laws in favour of her younger sister. When finally, her marriage takes place with the same man, she takes her revenge. 'Eyesore' is a story of a man whose wife runs away with one who was meant to safeguard her. The twist in the tale comes when the youngest daughter-in-law of the *zamindar* hears the news of the elopement. 'A New Tenant' is the story of a Nawab Sahab who shifts with his grown-up daughters to a new house. The beauty of the ladies attracts the attention of the youths and others. The charm of the story lies in the fact that nothing happens. Nawab Sahab leaves the place with his daughters to the frustrations of the youths. All three stories are marked by Premi's humour and wit. His power of observation regarding the smallest events of daily life was his greatest asset. The stories are short, with characters that Premi sketches in myriad colours like a painter. His characters make us believe they were next-door neighbours and yet seemed so removed.

Firoz Abid remains the senior-most writer and has been published in *Shab Khoon* and other journals in India. 'Scenes behind Scenes' is a depiction of the disturbances of the 1970s marked by senseless political killings. But it is an image of universal happenings that take place irrespective of time. The stark comparison of scenes of love and the killing of an innocent boy is a chilling reminder of the heartlessness of human society. 'Insight', a story from the book *Naqsh Bar Aab*, is a serious measure of the inadequacy of its time and a satire on human foibles. It is an amalgamation of the abstract and concrete through which the story leads us to some conclusion.

'A Story Heard Before' is a thriller-type narrative told by one character to another that ends on a note that could have been tragic. Two strangers meet amidst bad weather, become friends, only to know they belong to different countries and are sworn enemies. It shows how easily man's shifting priorities become their real adversaries. 'The Inner Fort' is one of the longest stories in this collection. Its length is closer to that of a novella. Anis Rafi takes us to a lost world of history, closer to fiction, and yet makes us wonder whether we have been mistakenly led to a past that almost existed. Written in ornate Urdu, with passion and wry humour, the characters remain etched in our memory long after the story ends.

Siddique Alam writes long stories, yet manages to keep the reader on tenterhooks. The two volumes of his stories have established his name as a short story writer in the country and abroad. 'The Stopped Clock' can be said to be his masterpiece. The beginning arrests the attention of the reader and the end of the story makes them wonder in amazement. It is more than a story. It is a criticism on the art of the short story itself. The story 'Agony' grips the attention of the reader from the opening lines. Strange as it seems, the protagonist receives a letter that informs him about his impending death. He does not die in the story, but his condition becomes worse than death. In this life-in-death situation, the protagonist learns, and the reader too, about the vicissitudes of life. 'The Wedding Register' takes us to a world that exists between reality and dreams. The protagonist, just like Alice in *Alice in Wonderland*, goes in search of a character that comes to life from an old, disused marriage register. They meet in a semi-supernatural environment, almost paranormal, but more than the character that he pursued, the protagonist meets his own self. When the protagonist comes back to his self, his daze is passed on to the readers. What takes place is the stuff that dreams and realities are made of.

The five stories of Mahmoud Yasien will appeal to emotions as well as the intellect. Most of Yasien's stories have been published in *Shab Khoon*, a literary Urdu journal that has published literary articles and short stories for decades. 'Arrival' is an example of the yearning in man, of something that remains mysterious, inexplicable, and thus, unattainable. 'Mr Storage' is another example of his obsession with dreams that are mixed with compassionate feelings towards a fellow writer of a foreign country. 'A Half-Serious Story' delves into the human psyche to show how words have a disturbing effect on the human mind. 'Psyche' leads to the world of dreams, where it is difficult to understand where vision starts and reality ends, but proves that dreams interpret life or that life may be stranger than dreams. 'Epic of the New Colony' is deceptive in its simplicity of straightforward narration. It is a multilayered narrative, an allegory that rises from the local to international level of politics and shows the domination of the powerful over the weak. It weaves a story of oppression to highlight the indomitable nature of the weak that refuses to surrender. From the micro to the macro and the topical levels, it is a story that establishes the unconquerable spirit of man.

Shahira Masroor is the only woman writer, and I wish I had accommodated more, for there is no dearth of women writers in the city. 'The Shop of Words' is unique in thought and content. Masroor, in a short span of this story, managed to merge the symbolic with the literal, the abstract with the concrete to lash at the inconsistencies of society.

Anisun Nabi's 'Similar' is a very different kind of story. It is based on a story of the Quran about the young men who were hounded by a despotic Roman ruler because of their religious beliefs. They were made to sleep in a cave for hundreds of years by God, only to wake up in a totally changed world. The story of these young men was also known to the Western world. John Donne had referred to the episode of the cave in one of his poems as the 'seven sleepers' den'. Although in the chapter *Surah Kahaf* of the Quran, this episode is mentioned, it does not go into the details, but Nabi has managed to add events and make the characters come alive in his story. He has also merged the ancient tale with the present times to make it topical. To enjoy the story, one is just required to suspend disbelief and move back and forth in time.

Reyaz Danish is the youngest amongst the writers. 'The Watch' and 'When Peace Came Around' are taken from his first collection *Jo Ama'a Mili*. 'The Watch' is a simple tale of a lost watch that leads to a misunderstanding between the son, daughter-in-law and the retired father who stays with them. The surprise ending reminds us of O. Henry's stories. 'When Peace Came Around' begins inside a religious place. It raises legitimate questions as to whether peace can ever be achieved for one whose soul is tainted with sin. Or, whether man can shake off his past under a new guise. It is the story of two battered souls, both suffering in their own cauldrons after committing an act of sin, which, once done, cannot be undone.

Shams Afif Siddiqi

WORKS CITED

1. Beg, Mirza Hamid. *Urdu Afsane Ki Rawayet*, 1903–1990. Islamabad: Academy Adibiyat Pakistan, Islamabad, 1991.
2. Faruqi, Shamsur Rahman. "Modern Urdu Literature". In *Modern Indian Literature: An Anthology. Vol 1: Surveys and Poems*, edited by K.M. George, 420–445. New Delhi: Sahitya Akademi, 1992.
3. Forster, E.M. *Aspects of the Novel.* New York: Rosetta Books, 2002.
4. Memon, Muhammad Umar. "Urdu Short Story: The Modernist Phase (1950s and After)". *Dawn*, May 25, 2014, https://www.dawn.com/news/1108350.
5. Reid, Ian. *The Short Story.* London and New York: Metheun, 1977.
6. Scofield, Martin, ed. *The Cambridge Introduction to the American Short Story*. Cambridge and New York: Cambridge University Press, 2006.
7. Zaidi, Ali Jawad. *A History of Urdu Literature*. Delhi: Sahitya Akademi, 1993.

THE DAWN OF REALISATION

SAYEED PREMI

It is unknown what dreams unmarried nights must have woven. Seema had affectionately kept them in some crevice of her imagination. Many a time, she used those dreams while combing and parting her hair like married women. Her body would be covered with dew-like drops.

'What do you dream all the time?' Her mother would admonish her. Seema would just smile.

Her friends also teased her. 'Who knows how many heartbeats you have increased?'

'One day a *swayamvar* will take place for you.'

'Nature has collected all the grace in one and named it Seema.'

Another colour was added to Seema's dreams, making her blush and go red in the face.

Seema was the daughter of Narendranath, the lawyer of the city civil court. She had completed her graduation. Her main subject was Philosophy. Her father loved her tremendously. She was not only simple in nature; her beauty carried the tone and tenor of innocence.

Meena was her younger sister, mischievous and naughty.

One evening, life sprinkled the seven colours of the rainbow on her. Seema blushed by herself. People had come to see her for marriage.

When her mother decked her up and handed her the tray, she failed to move her feet. Meena teased and whispered in her ears: '*Didi*! My would-be *jija* is handsome. I just had a look at him.'

That increased the heartbeats further. Strange whispers sounded in her ears. Her dreams were going to be realised.

Her mother said: 'Guests are waiting.'

She trudged to the room and unintentionally looked up. Two pairs of eyes had been staring at her. She hurriedly averted her eyes. But her heart, in that momentary flash, had built the foundation of a nest for herself. She could not tarry any longer. She does not remember how she managed to place the cups before the guests. When her mother brought her back, the desire to have a second look awakened in her heart. Coyness came in the way. She hurried straight to her room. Meena followed her.

'Isn't he handsome?'

'Naughty girl. Run away,' Seema said.

'Arrey *didi*. Why shy from me? After all, I too have a share in the stake.'

'Will you go away or I …' Seema lifted her hands playfully.

The guests had accepted the proposal.

Now the lonely hours became colourful. Time and again, only one face cropped up before her. She would smile, feel proud, at other moments, lie down; she travelled on the wings of clouds and reached imaginary heights. Stars would bow down, the moon would whisper in her ears, and passions melted to ooze out like perspiration. She would blush and feel tingles in her body. These open expressions of passion would create a storm within her. She would hurriedly come out from the world of her imagination.

Then something unexpected happened.

The people from the groom's side sent a reply.

Instead of Seema, they wanted to make her younger sister their daughter-in-law.

Seema felt something break inside her. The feeling was life-threatening.

Yearnings died on the threshold of dreams. Two wild eyes gazed at the destruction of a world that crumbled before it came into existence.

For a while, silence had overpowered the house. Sorrow was unbearable in silence. Uff! Why is no one talking? Why does no one scream? Why doesn't something break the piercing silence?

That silence ultimately came to an end. Seema heard the sound of her father's steps, hazy before it became clearer.

'They played a joke. They were interested in the elder. Now they want to make the younger one their daughter-in-law. How can they play with a person's feelings? They will have to accept Seema. I will not agree to any other proposal.'

The threat of the lawyer worked. They agreed to accept Seema. But the change of heart did not affect Seema at all. Her feelings remained stolid. The extinguished lamp of happiness refused to be ignited again.

The family members were content and happy. The lawyer was happy as if he had succeeded in saving his client from a death sentence. Seema felt a sense of defeat. She could not bear the affront. Many a time, the idea of rejecting the proposal came to her mind. She failed to say anything.

Then Seema soon became Mrs Kedarnath.

On the first night that would herald a new life, she took a strange decision.

When Kedarnath removed the veil from her face, it was devoid of coyness. She looked straight into his eyes and said: 'Only before the world are we husband and wife.'

Kedarnath was not prepared for such words. Still, he acted with restraint and replied: 'Seema, I know the reason for your displeasure. I had no hand in it. My mother took the decision.'

'You should have taken it,' Seema was straightforward.

'I did not have the courage to go against my mother.'

'You proved your cowardice,' she said

'Seema, please forget the past. I am with you.'

Seema was not ready for any explanation. She was prepared to face life in her way.

Kedarnath accepted life as it came his way. He accepted Seema's wishes as his own. There was a prospect of a transfer, and it was a ray of hope. Staying away from family members might help him come close to his wife.

But it failed to bring a smile on Kedarnath's face. No change took place in Seema.

Kedarnath tried his best to prove himself a good husband. He would give his full salary to her and request the amount he needed for himself. He would spend on her whatever extra he managed to earn. He would buy her new saris, make-up and take her out to see films.

Sometimes he thought she was punishing him for the sin he had not committed. At other times, reason would advise acting against circumstance, but practical sense made him desist. He would just stare lovingly at her face. He did not want to put further pressure on her. He wanted to win her with care and love.

These were moments of trial for Seema. The love in the eyes of Kedarnath would shake the foundation of her resolve. She wanted to play naughty tricks on him. The love of Kedarnath made her believe how unjust she had been with him. She knew love had overtaken her. In such moments she wanted to rush to him, embrace and say: 'I have lost. Take me in your embrace.'

But then the past would return, making her put the mask on her face.

She started caring for him. Kedarnath got whatever he needed. If he suffered physical pain, she would be up for the whole night. If guests arrived, she would present such a show of filial bond that Kedarnath was amazed. Apparently, when they seemed to have everything, in reality they did not. A year passed, and up came the marriage anniversary. Kedarnath made plans for the celebration but desisted seeing his wife's indifference.

When Kedarnath came out of his office, there were marks of tension on his face. He walked the street, oblivious of the surroundings. There was a sense of hollowness in him. Strange thoughts crowded his mind, half-baked thoughts that led to Seema. Everything looked hazy. Soon at a crossing, he thought he heard a din and clash. He could not remember what had happened after that. He had come under the wheels of a bus.

Seema, meanwhile, impatiently waited for his arrival. Kedarnath had never been late before. Strange thoughts were making her restless. For the first time, she knew that without Kedarnath, she was incomplete. Just a delay of one or two hours had taken away her pride. Restlessness had taken hold of her.

It was at eight at night when news reached her. Kedarnath was admitted to the Nanavati Hospital. The news was like lightning. It tore her existence into pieces.

Seema was running on the streets like a mad woman.

EYESORE

SAYEED PREMI

The arrival of the letter created a storm in the village. From Satgaon, Ramdayal Kumhar's brother-in-law had written that Rukmini had not yet reached her mother's house.

Sometimes Ramdayal would look at Bansi Thakur, who by now had read the letter thrice; sometimes the letter was stuck in between his fingers and sometimes the person who had brought it—was Bansi joking? The bloody idiot is a comedian, who knows, he might have included the man in his plan that brought the letter?

'Forget joking,' he said. 'Read the letter properly and say what is written in it.'

Bansi Thakur looked at Ramdayal with sad eyes. 'Is it the time for a joke? You have heard what is written in the letter.'

One, two, three, four, eight, ten; people slowly started gathering around Ramdayal. Everyone who arrived there would curiously ask the reason for the assembly and after getting to know, stare at Ramdayal with strange looks. Ramdayal felt as if he was standing naked on the Cross of the air and people were piercing every part of his body with the nails of their looks: slanted nails, skewed ones, hard ones, soft ones, and he, instead of blood, was bathed in sweat.

Somebody called from the crowd: 'Didn't Rukmini go to her mother's place with Dinanath?'

'Yes. Dinanath had taken Rukmini there.'

'Rukmini and Dinanath.'

'Dinanath and Rukmini.'

A voice came from amongst the crowd: 'Dinanath had eloped with Rukmini.'

Suddenly there was silence; it seemed that there was nobody, none, only black, brown, small, big eyes staring at each other, as if trying to ascertain the truth of the spoken word that now travelled far on the wings of the air—but each eye unable to understand the other, making Ramdayal feel out of breath; silence was piercing every part of his body, crushing his soul.

Oh! This silence! Why is nobody talking? Why is nobody laughing? What kind of villagers are these people? Why is nobody making fun of him? Then like a volcano that had been dormant inside the earth, he burst open. 'Yes, my Rukmini has eloped… my wife has run away… Dinanath has run away with her…'

He ran towards his house like a mad man. People saw him ruthlessly pick up the plates and throw them away; plates that he had laboured hard to make throughout the year, to be sold at the fair, and on which beautiful flowers and leaves had been engraved. Before Bansi Thakur could catch hold of his walking stick and reach there, Ramdayal had already broken more than half the plates. A strange frenzy had taken hold of him. Bansi Thakur took hold of his hand and said: 'Have you gone mad or what? Why are you destroying the fruits of your hard labour?'

'For whom should I save these Bansi, when Rukmini herself has gone away?'

Leaning on the shoulders of Bansi Thakur, he cried like a child. Feeling the pain of his childhood friend, Bansi Thakur's eyes too got wet. He tried to console him but his voice got stuck in his throat. He slowly patted the shoulders of his friend. If the sorrow oozes away, it's better…

That day an unusual crowd had gathered at the community space. The discussion veered around only one topic: Dinanath had eloped with Rukmini. Today no one was interested in the concocted tales of old Banwari, neither was anyone interested in the stories about the city from Sukhdeo, nor did they request Chandu Kaka for Mira's *bhajan*. What's more, no one looked towards Dinu Patwari's Moradabadi *hukkah* with greedy eyes, from which emitted the aroma of Lucknawi tobacco. There was only one point of discussion: Rukmini had eloped. Dinanath had run away with her.

Dinu Patwari was feeling insulted because of the lack of interest in his Moradabadi *hukkah*. He took a long tug to reinforce its importance. That made him cough. Somehow, he tried to control his cough and said: 'Chaudhury! It is amazing to think what Dinanath saw in Rukmini, that he fell for her? She was dark like the new moon night, the vile woman!'

Chaudhury, who had been quiet till now, twitched his moustache for some time, changed the shape of his lips, moved his hands on his starched headgear, played his fingers on his snuff box, but without opening it kept it back in his pocket. All eyes were on him expecting something that probably no one knew. Chaudhury, understanding the momentary importance of his self, cleared his throat and said: 'Arrey Dinu! This is something about the heart.'

Chaudhury said this and became silent. Others were disappointed with this short reply. But Chaudhury got lost in some moments of the past. Rukmini was at the grinding wheel. The fish-like parts of her exposed flesh were dancing with the movement of her body. The *aanchal*, part of the sari to cover the body, had never been in her control. Despicable woman! Her body was unbelievably taut! Like a sack of English mud.

He pulled down the towel from his shoulders and wiped his mouth, a deep anger against the world rose in his mind.

'This wicked Dinanath tried to pass off like a good man,' broke in the old Panwari. 'He has robbed the village of its honour. Let me get hold of him, Chaudhury. Then I will show him what I can do.'

Then others joined in and a flood of voices drowned the place.

That night some untoward things happened in the village. Sarju, who would come late at night drunk and thrash his wife, sat quietly on the threshold in the dark and stared into nothingness; moments of the bloody past can kill. His wife came out many a times; probably the woman in her was out to revolt.

The house light of the Numbardar, the prominent president of the village, instead of being switched off at the earliest, remained lit the whole night. Light also tends to keep a watch. It is possible that the darkness could devour the 16-year-old wife of this 50-year-old man. The village dogs that itched to bark the whole night, and disturb the sleep of the villagers, were lying peacefully. Dogs are really faithful. Dukhiya Mousi, a tuberculosis patient, who usually coughed the whole night long, was singing in her feeble voice. Past memories remain like dying embers or, maybe, the heart never becomes old.

Ramdayal with bowed head sat near his spinning wheel. Today he did not even light the lantern he had bought with such fondness from the town. Days are like birds; they do not come back. Every single thought was breaking down like pieces of glass, spreading out strands of memories, bruising the mind. Ramdayal tried to break free from the fetters of the past, but the walls of its prison were too high to be scaled. He stood before the threshold of moments, staring into time past, and his eyes became wet. His tears mingled with the shadows, spread all over, made the darkness depressing. All over, the silence was like the terrible stillness of the burning *ghat*; only the whizzing sound of the wind, like the curves in Rukmini's body, was piercing the body of Ramdayal. He was constantly moving his hands on his body as if it was not his own.

The next day, there was an unusual crowd at the well, but nobody was in a hurry. No quarrel ensued over the change of the positions of utensils, before or after, at the queue near the well. Nor did anyone, like on usual days, accuse the daughter of Sukhiya Dai, wife of Dinu Patwari, of stealing in the fields in the evening and later getting released also. Nor did anyone try to build mountains out of molehills about the happenings at the *zamindar*'s *haveli*. There was only one topic of discussion that held sway.

'What came into the mind of that vile Rukmini?'

'Arrey, imagine what a hypocrite that Dinanath turned out to be?'

'How innocent that depraved man pretended to be?'

'What priceless quality did he find in Rukmini that he ran away with her?'

'Can anyone fall for such a dark, base woman?'

'Shame on them! What sin have they committed together!'

'I had known it the day this Dinanath had come to the village.'

Who was this Dinanath? Where did he come from? Nobody knew. Everyone had summed up some opinion about him in their own way. Dinanath too had never told anyone about himself. His house was to the east where a rivulet flowed by, which he had bought from the younger brother of Banwari. Whether his arrival to the village was liked or not by others, the spinsters were overjoyed. And, under almost every roof of the village an unmarried dream was being cherished. After that even the middle-aged women were seen lining up to gather water from the well. The youngsters had to go over to the rivulets.

Dinanath really looked like a prince of some unseen land. Tall, well-built and broad chested, he had curls falling down his shoulders, brown eyes, and a nose fair and chiselled like the hills.

With the passage of time, everyone became close to him. There was no one in the village who had not become indebted to Dinanath for something or the other. He was courteous and mixed freely with people. If anyone needed some help, he would unhesitatingly knock at his door. Dinanath would immediately get up to help without a thought.

Then a time came when the villagers developed such faith in the man that they even had no hesitation in sending their daughters-in-law to their mothers' houses and back home with him, without any hesitation. Ramdayal too had sent Rukmini with Dinanath to Satgaon.

This news soon reached even the *haveli* of the *zamindar*. The youngest daughter-in-law had at that time just come out of her bath. She was drying out her long, soft tresses with a towel. Some drops of water on her beautiful, moon-like face sparkled like gems. The brownish-yellow cotton sari with red edges clung to parts of her body.

When the youngest daughter-in-law heard the news, her hand suddenly stopped. Her face became flushed, maybe because of anger or a sense of defeat. The only word that she was capable of uttering was: 'Rascal.'

Dinanath had once taken the youngest daughter-in-law to her mother's house as well.

A NEW TENANT

SAYEED PREMI

A new tenant arrived at the house of Haji Karim Buksh. It seemed spring had quietly invaded the whole *mohalla*.

The new tenant was Nawab Bedar Bakht. His personality evoked a sense of dignity. He was more than six feet tall, with broad shoulders, a straight neck, bushy brows, and a face with an air of self-esteem.

But the spring that arrived at the *mohalla* was not because of the grand persona of the man. He had four daughters whom God must have created in his leisure. If one was like the poem of Faiz, the other, a ghazal of Riaz. If the third was the *Rubaiyat* of Khayyam, the other a song of Tagore.

The house of Haji Karim Buksh was situated on a street that looked like a lane. Opposite the house was Firdaus Variety Store, close to it, a *paan* shop, a *Cuttacki* masala-*wala*, and a bit removed, a tea shop that, more or less, remained closed. Next was the shop of a washerman, where the clothes of almost all young men of the area were washed. Further away from the washerman sat a seller of fruits. Then there was the meat shop, whose owner was infamous for weighing less and charging more. There was also a grocer, a tailor, and a masjid. After the masjid, the street turned to its left.

Opposite to the store were Arrow Tailoring and the Hindu grocer, from where people took things on credit. There was the godown of old tyres, a shop that sold tea without sugar, a snack shop that used cheap oil and where the young men with nothing to do crowded all the time. Though this hampered his business, the owner remained tight-lipped, for if he protested, he would lose the little money that came his way. He could also get one or two blows in exchange. There was also Shamim Eating House, the owner in the cashier's seat interested in singing panegyrics against his workers. There was the Ladies Tailor that usually catered to Anglo-Indian ladies. His shop was the source of attraction. Passers-by would not forget to throw a casual glance—at the fine fabrics, as well as the exposed parts of the fair ladies. There was also a bald doctor followed by two more shops when the lane turned towards the main road.

Amongst them, now Firdaus Variety Store had acquired importance, its income increasing unexpectedly. Outside the store, there was a long, cemented platform. It was hardly used. The itch-prone dogs of the *mohalla* would lie there, spreading out their legs. The owner of the store would drive them away whenever he stepped out. The dogs, to be on the safe side, would walk away when they saw the owner. They would return when the danger was over.

But now, the original claimant of the platform had been driven out permanently. If some vocal ones amongst the dogs tried to lay claim, the buddies would beat them in such a way that they would never be seen for days. The weak or timid ones never even came that way. Now, this platform had acquired the position of eminence. The youths would shift-wise occupy seats, that is, one shift for the morning, noon, and afternoon, and another for the evening. The evening shift was of significance because that included students of schools and colleges from well-to-do families.

The store owner gained a great deal from the evening shift. He sold the customers things at exorbitant rates. The youth understood his fraudulence yet, gladly allowed him to pick holes in their pockets. As if occupying a seat on the platform to catch a glimpse of beauty was like paying a tax in advance. This was not a big deal, for after every one or two days, the glimpse of unveiled beauty would quench the thirst of their restless, passionate eyes. The four sisters would come around, accompanied either by the Nawab Sahab or by themselves. Those moments were breathtakingly wonderful. From one end to the other, spectators stood, holding their breaths at the spectacle.

The Gujarati owner of Firdaus Store would clean the glasses of his much-cleaned spectacles and put them on. Outside on the platform, the youths would suddenly turn dignified, conscious about gender in the use of words. The *Cuttacki* masala-*wala* would hurriedly bring down to the knees his dhoti, dirtier than the dusting cloth; the Shamim Store owner turned decent, the bald doctor, without rhyme and reason, would stand near the door of his dispensary and wash his hands.

And those beautiful ladies, that are the enemies of faith, would move out of sight briskly—and come to an end within the flash of a moment. The monotony of life returns once again; the momentary gaiety of life on the lane suddenly turns deserted.

The relationship between longing for the damsels and their physical appearance would go on throughout the day. Thus, six months passed since Nawab Sahab came to our *mohalla*. In this period, Nawab Sahab had personally come to know many people of the area, and most of them were youths.

Then something strange happened. For a week, neither the daughters of Nawab Sahab came on the balcony nor did they venture out of the house. This, especially for those perched on the platform near Firdaus Store, was of extreme torment. Their topic of discussion veered only on this.

'What's the matter?' Rahim's son, Jamil, asked thoughtfully.

'Maybe Nawab Sahab might have imposed restrictions,' Sultan replied. The youth had come from another *mohalla* to try his luck here. He was a friend of Jamil.

'I think something is wrong,' Rizwan broke in. His father had died recently, leaving huge property. That is why his social status had become uplifted. He was a final-year student but only in name. After his father's death, he was free to choose his way. Life taught him things much earlier. Rizwan then added: 'Can it be...' but stopped midway.

Eyes stared, expecting some resolution of the mystery. But silence ensued; the restlessness increased. Some questioning voices arose, and Rizwan remained tight-lipped. Others tried to find answers in the half statement. Rizwan did not complete the statement but immediately left the place. Sultan looked towards Jamil and vice versa. Both were unable to find the meaning that lay behind the stare. Then all left, one after the other.

Rizwan's incomplete statement had put a stamp on their lips.

The owner of Firdaus Store peeped at the empty platform, then stared at the building of Haji Karim Buksh. His eyes were full of sorrow. He took up a piece of cloth to clean the showcase. But soon, a thought struck. He took up a bucket of water and angrily sprinkled it on the cemented platform.

The next day something created a furore.

People saw a jeep of the D.C., D.D., and a large police van outside the building of Haji Karim Buksh. The police had encircled the house from all sides.

Nawab Sahab was coming out of the building with his daughters.

SCENES BEHIND SCENES

FIROZ ABID

My son was awake in his cradle.

My wife, I do not know for how long, had been rocking the cradle to make him fall asleep. I, in my bed, wallowing in the smoke of my cigarette, was relishing, musing about the curves of my wife's body.

'Shanti, come along, the rascal won't sleep,' the relish had permeated my voice.

'Coming, don't be impatient. The night is still young. He will start crying if I leave him.' My wife's voice was loaded with love and motherly affection.

My mother was lying awake in the adjacent room. She was talking to Krishan, the younger son of my elder brother. In the next room, my elder brother and sister-in-law were also wide awake for the light of their room was still on.

The sound of a bomb bursting came from afar. My son gave a start and my wife started her lullaby. My wife went on with her lullaby. My son was still awake. My mother was also wide awake. My elder brother and his wife were also awake and then the sound of the bursting of bombs increased with leaps and bounds.

My elder brother's son fell asleep.

My mother fell asleep.

Elder brother and his wife fell asleep.

The bombings went on and the whole *mohalla* was in the lap of sound sleep. Then my wife came around to me. Her eyelids carried the telltale marks of approaching weary slumber.

'He finally slept. Your lullaby has a sweet melody,' I said kissing her tresses.

'Not my voice. It was the sound of the bombings that appeared sweet to him and he fell asleep.' My wife got entangled in my clutches and when morning dawned, I saw that she remained tangled in the same way. It was approaching 10 o'clock. I had to hurry to my office for the statement had to be readied.

I reached Sealdah.

Blamb!

Blamb!

Blamb!

With the sound of bombings, a sea of humanity could be seen. Everyone was questioning the other.

'What happened? Why did it happen?

Near Surendranath College, on Mahatma Gandhi Road, three trams were set on fire.

Naxalbari *Lal Salaam.*

Lal Salaam.

The words were neither romantic nor carried faith, but momentary passion had mixed with the sound.

Tear gas had started to make its presence felt in my eyes. I soaked my handkerchief from the nearby road tap and squeezed it on my eyes.

'Move, please move, he won't survive... will die!' many voices were hovering in the air.

I saw a boy in dirty attire, soaked in blood.

He was shot by the police. He was hardly 14 years old.

'How was he shot?' a voice rose against all the others.

'He worked in a tea stall. He was young; went inside the crowd. He got shot.'

The voice carried the pain of the love for life.

The next day the newspaper carried the headline: 'A Naxalbari student shot dead by police on Mahatma Gandhi Road.'

INSIGHT

FIROZ ABID

Then everyone's eyes widened with surprise, and again, hue and cry began. The group leader was convinced that it was the spot where his officer had asked them to assemble and wait. But the sign that was given, which he had identified before, and remained important, was missing. It could not be found anywhere, though other things were intact. But how was that possible? How can such a huge statue vanish from the spot? He failed to understand how the statue, its platform, the circular area, flowers, and giant-sized lamps, were all missing. Only the dusty and uneven land remained. So how did it happen? His thoughts, dashing against the borders of thoughtlessness, were getting hazy. His confusion was increasing with the sounds of the uproar. He failed to understand his next plan of action. At this point, a man, advanced in age, came up and asked which way they should proceed. The man's face had the impression of a lengthy journey of life and centuries of cruel sadness. Behind him were an old lady, a middle-aged woman, and a boy. The old lady's eyes neither had the sadness nor the impression of centuries of sorrow. Her creased face carried a sense of peace. The middle-aged woman's face was free from all these. Only her eyes stared at the moving lips of the old lady. At times, she swallowed something that seemed like her own voice. The young boy had expectant eyes. The turmoil in his eyes searched for the shadow of peace.

The leader of the group was quiet. Men, women, and children stood in a queue, from one point to the other. To break the silence, the boy said: 'Babu, take me to the statue. One of the legs had broken. To repair it, experts had spent days and evenings in discussion. Money was collected. It was repaired. Yet the flaw remained.'

The leader remained quiet and began to ponder. The clamour increased. Many voices now took the form of sentences to reach his ears. Every sentence was the opposite of the other. They were impassive and inconsiderate. Every sentence was free from time, circumstances, necessity, and the present. The leader's thoughts had taken a new direction. Now he found deceit, betrayal, and falsehood in everything. He was feeling a sense of dislike for everyone, including himself.

The young boy again asked: 'Babu! Where are those gun-toting guards? They were supposed to guard the statue so that the second leg does not get broken. Day before yesterday, the village headman said that the statue was that of a man of great ahimsa.'

'Be quiet!' He cast a strict glance at the boy. 'You know nothing.'

'That is why we are asking. Where is the statue? Show us.'

The leader wanted to say that he himself did not know, but he failed. For the truth is fearless. If he showed fearlessness, then the unmindful and unemotional sentences may join together. His leadership will come under the ambit of thoughts.

The sun was getting warmer. The dust was piercing his eyes.

The young boy entered amidst the crowd. He asked the same question to his father.

His father, a middle-aged man whose eyes carried the impression of a long journey and cruel sadness, failed to reply, and just gulped down phlegm. The old lady addressed the boy with composure: 'Boy! Sit somewhere in the shade. Don't loiter in the sun.'

The young boy smilingly looked towards his grandmother and said: 'Grandma, you used to tell me many stories and you still remember them. All the stories were tales of happiness and sadness, joy and sorrow, wealth and poverty. You placed importance on jubilation and contentment. Grandma, all your stories were false.'

The elderly lady gazed at her grandson. Maybe he might not have understood. It was then that the middle-aged woman, whose face had a sense of calm, told her son: 'Why don't you listen to Grandma? Go and splash water on your face. Why are you worried?'

The young boy smiled: 'Ma, do you know stories that end in joy and happiness? You never told me stories. You are asking me to splash water. Grandma wants me to sit in the shade. This town has neither shade nor water.'

The middle-aged woman glanced at her son as if she had understood everything and as if she understood nothing. She looked towards her husband, who was explaining something to people. Her gaze, like earlier, was fixed on the half-open lips of her husband.

The leader was nowhere to be seen, neither near nor afar, neither in the crowd nor alone. People were restless, engaged in the chaotic hue and cry. Their voices were cold and quiet. After some time, the leader's face was spotted. He asked the people to follow him. They looked upon him as a support and walked on. The uneven road of the town, its slippery coal tar, the shadowless and tall buildings, fast-moving vehicles, buses, hand rickshaws, dust and dirt, and directionless voices. People walked on; old, middle-aged, young men and women, young boys and girls.

The leader made them stand in a queue. Faraway, thousands stood in the sprawling *maidan*. The words and suitable sentences of the leader failed to appeal to their ears.

Every eye gazed at the polythene packets that the leader was distributing. Hunger could be seen on their lips.

Suddenly the sky turned dark. A light breeze started to blow. The words of the speaker were quivering in the wind. The light breeze took the form of a storm. The women tried to hide their children somehow but proved ineffective. There was no sign of a shelter.

The speakers were safe inside the *shamiana*. To save their vision, thousands had closed their eyes.

The storm was raging.

Everywhere there was a dark silence.

Then the lightning struck. The drizzle gave way to torrential rain. In the huge sprawling *maidan*, where thousands of people had collected got drenched.

Everywhere there was a dark silence.

The rising, drowning voices. Voices in thousands. Directionless voices.

Drenched people, running people, skyscrapers, shadowless buildings, old, tough legs, exhausted, middle-aged legs, young legs, bathed in voices of different colours. Direction, directionless.

North, south, east, and west, men were moving in large numbers. The mad wind was blowing. The rain was under the influence of the wind and a victim of being erratic.

Crowds of men; crowded dreams.

Crowds and crowds of wishes.
The silence of the leaders.
The call of the leaders.
Light, devoid of insight.
North, south, east and west—right and left.
A cover of different colours on the vision of the crowd.
Which colour is the truth?
Which is false?
Or, all are false!

A STORY HEARD BEFORE

ANIS RAFI

M.V.S. Murthy was looking out of the right window screen of the car. Every scene was manifesting new impressions on his face, even though travel was a part of his official duty. He would usually travel in deserted mountainous regions. I was travelling for the first time with him. I never liked travelling quietly. I wanted Murthy to tell me in detail about mica and the mountains where acid was found. When I smoked too many cigarettes and the smoke affected his eyes, he turned to me.

'We government servants have to be at all sorts of places.'

'It's nothing new. And it does not matter whether you are from Tamil Nadu and I'm from Bengal.'

'What do you mean?'

'I just want to ask you how far away we are from the mountains on which I will be making the documentary.'

'Thirty-two kilometres.'

'Murthy, I had heard that Alchemists are nutty, they talk less, but you…'

'I search for acids in the mountains. I know there are too much in these mountains. The chemistry in which acid was assimilated was derived from the Germans. In my student days, I wondered why the amalgamation could not be made in our country that produced acid. I was a student of Chemistry. It got stuck somewhere in my mind, and when I got employed in the chemical exploration department, the idea was still there. I was posted in Pathankot in those days where the chemical exploration was being undertaken. There is still 20 kilometres left to be covered, if you want, I can tell you a story. It was told to me by an army friend of mine. He was Colonel Rawat, from Bhubaneshwar, Orissa.

'Okay. That would pass the time.'

Murthy started his tale.

It was a tale that took place around Pathankot. The condition was not well at the borders. Time and again, the sounds of shell fire could be heard. Both parties were hell bent on firing artillery shells on each other. The condition was really serious. It must have been six in the evening. The sky was overcast, which was also an indication that conditions could worsen. It had started to drizzle. The signs of thundershowers were beginning to emerge. Silence had enveloped the whole place. As far as the eye could see, silence had covered the highway. The movement of traffic had virtually come to a stop. Far away in the distance, the city lights were blinking lazily.

Amidst the dim and hazy highway lights stood a banyan tree at the far end. A man stood under this tree. He wore an overcoat. He was a bit drenched, and was trying to save himself from the falling rain. The air had also become cool. The downpour was turning into a storm. Maybe somewhere low air pressure must have formed. The TV report had stated that there may be a hailstorm in and around the Kashmir valley.

The man had put his hands inside the coat pockets in order to ward off the cold. The mercury kept on sliding and a cold shower fell in torrents. There was no chance of its abating. Slowly the shower precipitated.

It was at this time that another man got down from his motorbike and sought refuge under the banyan tree. Now two men were taking shelter under the tree. The thunderous lightning had reached its peak. The two stared at each other, and then at the leaves of the tree, as if expressing gratitude for providing shelter. The cold wind continued to blow.

The man in the overcoat brought out a cigarette from his pocket, possibly the last one left. The man who had got down from the motorbike, understood his predicament.

He said: 'Sir! You need a matchbox. I have it with me.'

The man handed the matchbox to the other.

'Thank you. It's really cold. My fingers have turned numb,' and he tried to open the matchbox. 'Ah! There is only one matchstick left in it.'

'I see. Now I must also light mine,' said the other and took out his cigarette from the pocket.

'Brother, you try it,' and he lit it with some effort. One end got lit and he quickly started tugging. When he was confident that the lighted cigarette would not be extinguished, he handed it to the other.

'Take it. It's yours.'

'No Sir, you carry on, I will light mine.' They both came close to one another.

'Why thank me? By handing me your matchbox you have helped me in this cold weather.'

'My God! In this cigarette and match talk, we have forgotten even to ask each other's name.'

'I am Nand Kishore, from Chandigarh. I had come here on business. My taxi broke down. I am now stuck here.'

'I am Vikram. I have a farmhouse, some 10 kilometres from here.'

'It's nice Vikram Sahab. We met here. I am new to this place. I was in fact feeling lonely.'

'Don't bother. I am a local. But it is not safe to stay here for long. You know how disturbed the border area is. Intruders come from all sides and spread terrorist activities.'

'You are right. What do think about the neighbouring country?'

'Brother, we are civilians. Why should we be bothered about these things? It is becoming cold and the cigarette is also in its last stage. As far as the neighbouring country is concerned, both the countries should adhere to their mutual agreement. After all, agreements are there to be followed.'

'Vikram Sahab. These are political matters. They are beyond our understanding. What we get in return is just confusion and that is our problem. What do you say?'

'You are 100 per cent correct. No one is bothered about others. Everyone is interested in himself.'

There was a sudden streak of lightning. The wind directed the shower towards the banyan tree and for a few minutes there was complete silence.

'The rain won't stop Vikram Sahab. The condition of the sky above and the ground below does not seem to augur well. The thunderstorm is at its peak. It's better if we leave this place, even though it is risky.'

'Let the rain abate a bit.'

'Okay. But where can we go. I am totally new to this place.'

'I told you I have a small farmhouse here. We will go there. Yashwant is there. He will prepare some dish for us.'

'God is great. He sends someone or the other for help. It seems that the rain is abating.'

Both the men had by this time got totally drenched.

'Okay let us move. This is the right time.'

'Come, let's go. We will reach the farmhouse in about 10 minutes.'

'This is your generosity, sir.'

'You be my pillion rider. Carry your suitcase in one hand, and with the other hold on to me. It is pitch dark. The road is also not in a good shape.'

Both took their seats on the motorbike. The old military disposal bike swiftly proceeded on its way. It stopped near the gate of a house. A man opened the door at the sound of the bike's horn. He helped the vehicle on its stand.

'Didn't I tell you not to venture out? But no one listens to me. See how you have got drenched. Who is this stranger with you?'

'Ramu Kaka, had I not gone out, how would I have brought this stranger home? We'll spend the night together. It would be great if you make some chicken dishes. It will put life into us.'

Ramu Kaka opened the door. The room was well furnished. There were four chairs, a table, and carpet on the floor.

'It's a nice and warm room.'

'Take rest. Be comfortable. These are clothes for you. There is an attached bathroom. Wash and change. Till then, I will be back.'

Both had changed when Ramu Kaka laid the bottle of rum, salad and other accessories on the table.

'Do you drink Mr Nand Kishore?'

'Not regularly, but sometimes I do. This is the appropriate occasion. The weather is also congenial for it.'

'It's good. I usually don't drink alone. Let us make the day memorable. This bottle is from the army,' he points to the rum bottle, 'you have no idea of the army. We somehow manage it from them. This is original. Many duplicates are available in the market.'

After two rounds of drinks, both became inebriated.

'Tell me something about your family, Mr Nand Kishore?

'Forget about family. Let us enjoy the drink.'

'Still…'

'Okay. I'll tell you about my family if that interests you. I am away from home for a week. My wife, your *bhabi*, is very beautiful. She is also a nice person. She is a mother of two and yet looks like a teenager. Romantic…'

'My wife too is just like that. When I was leaving to come here, there were tears in her eyes. She prayed for my safe return. I have two kids. Both are girls. They too are very beautiful. But I do not know for what mistake God has punished me.'

'What do you mean?'

'One suffers from polio and the other is dumb,' he bent a bit and a moan escaped as if something had got stuck in his throat. He sobbed for a while.

'I am sorry. It has affected me deeply.' He brought the man closer and tried to console him.

They soon partook of the delicious chicken to their heart's content.

'We have met by accident, Vikram Sahab. Though the weather was bad, the manner in which I was welcomed here will be memorable. I thank you for your warm hospitality. Come, let us embrace each other with affection.'

They warmly hugged each other. Their conversation inched on further, with rum and chicken.

'If you don't mind, can I use your toilet please?'

'Sure!'

Nand Kishore went inside the toilet. Vikram noticed the man's suitcase. Curiosity made him think of opening it, and he did. It carried a sign. The man was a spy. Vikram took out his pistol and stood near the closed toilet door. Nand Kishore heard the sound of the opening of his suitcase. He also brought out his pistol that was fastened to his waist. Both were wary of the other. Their blood pressure increased due to fear and tension. Faces were flushed with anger. Just a few minutes ago they had been so friendly. As soon as the door opened Vikram held his pistol at Nand Kishore.

'Hands up,' they screamed together. They came close to each other as at the time of embracing. The only difference was now they pointed pistols at each other's head.

'Vikram Sahab, I knew you must be a Major. Do you know when? When you opened the bottle of rum. Those are meant only for army officers. Don't you pull the trigger Major! Yes, I am a spy. But I do not want to die so easily. I want to live for the sake of my children. Let me leave. Please give me the way.'

'You cannot leave. I am a Major. I am a patriot and an army officer. You are not my friend anymore. I will prove my love for my country.'

'What will you get by exterminating me? Just a few minutes ago we were friends! How can we suddenly turn into enemies? Don't you pull the trigger? We both will die. The blood that will flow will be a stain on our friendship. In this cold weather, when everything is freezing, your wife will miss your warm kisses. She will become a widow.'

'So what? She will be looked after by my motherland. She will be awarded a posthumous award also.'

The headlines will say that two men died. No one will say when, where, and how we met before dying. If you want to die, I will count from ten to one, backwards. You can then pull the trigger. Ready!'

'Before beginning the countdown, I am giving you another chance. Decide.'

'I have decided. If you are not beginning the count, then I will...'

'Ten, nine, eight ...'

Whether the countdown was completed or not, Murthy became quiet. He looked serious and stared out of the windscreen of the car. The acid mountain appeared close by. He turned around and looked at me. Except for the professional curiosity there was nothing in my eyes. But what I saw in Murthy's eyes, made me sit up.

The car was slowly moving by the edges of the acid-bearing mountains.

THE INNER FORT

ANIS RAFI

His destination was the inner fort. In the list of his orders, it was only stated that the 'inner fort' lay on the outskirts of the city of Bahadurabad. But on arriving there, he faced a problem. This was the anonymity of the inner fort. It was difficult to find anyone who had proper knowledge of the place. The political affairs department also had no information about its existence. The professionals in the tourism industry were possibly uninterested in such ruins because they were not profitable. Now he was feeling annoyed with his managing director who was an elderly lady. His first assignment after his appointment was becoming difficult and unexciting. But she had insisted that the inner fort be found. If the firm managed to complete the job, it would prove to be highly profitable for them. She would not accept that the inner fort did not exist. It was the firm's job to find new sites. Oil firms had managed to discover oil in all sorts of places: forests, mountains, oceans, everywhere. Compared to those, the inner fort was situated in a convenient location. The employees of the company had to comply with the decision taken by her. So, the job of the discovery of the unknown, remote, and mysterious fort was handed to him. He could not refuse, for it was his first assignment order from the office. He was appointed for such kinds of projects. The discovery of archaeological sites was a subject of special interest for him. It was his specialisation in his MA degree. During the selection process for the job, he was given preference over others because of this.

He reached Bahadurabad without much difficulty. It is a historical place. People here are cultured. But their ignorance of the inner fort is distressing. They cannot be blamed; after all, the inner fort is not the full fort. It may not even be half. Probably, it played no role in the daily life of the city of Bahadurabad, or else people would have remembered it. It was possible that the 'inner fort' also had an outer fort. There is no visible sign of that, nor do people talk about it. The only known geographical location is that the fort lies one-and-a-quarter kilometres south of the city end. Nothing is known about its *mohalla*, block, *tehsil*, or subdivision. On enquiries about its location, some thought it prudent only to smile. One of them questioned the name itself. The city, according to him, should have been called Bhoj Rajpur. Maharajkumar Rana had given refuge to Prince Bahadur Khan, treated him as his guest, as well as saved his life. Rana Bhoj Raj named this city Bahadurabad. This kind of hospitality had never been heard of before. So why can we not remember this great predecessor and rename Bahadurabad as Ranarajpur? That was a strange kind of logic. Different kinds of men have different philosophies. Some men shook off the chains of the past, some broke them, while others repaired them. He was left surprised and exasperated. To him, the whole exercise seemed like an Archaeology class was going on; he, like a village simpleton, was just forced to gape and listen in awe. He wanted to say that he had no interest in the tales of valour or craftiness of either Prince Bahadur Khan or his father, Muzaffar Shah. His curiosity was only confined to the inner fort. He wanted some clue that could lead him to his destination for which he had been deputed. Though he had expressed his objective, everyone was only interested in the expression of his own opinion. Each man thinking that his view was superior to others. An ordinary subject was here made complicated; he was face-to-face with strange men. Mischief mongering was at its peak; he was reduced to looking around helplessly. How long will he go on moving aimlessly! Whether it was Muzaffarabad, or Bahadurabad, he was not staking any claim over it. If it was Bahadurabad, so be it! Why should it be rejected? Every place had its own sanctity. What did not exist, or had been lost, or could be lost, at least a search should be conducted. He just wanted a clue to the whereabouts of the inner fort. By imposing new demands, a lot of things may slip away. Were these ignorant men aware of that?

He was aimlessly roving along. Then it must have been a godsend. A hackney-carriage driver, dressed in rags, came along the way from the Company Park end. Till now, he had not come across any *tonga, tumtum, ekka,* or even a hand-drawn rickshaw in this town. The sudden appearance of the *tongawallah* made him holler after him. The call made the driver shudder, but he pulled the reins of the horse to stop it. The *bidi* dropped from his jaws and fell on the road.

'Sir! I carry goods, not passengers. The auto stand is close by.'

The panic of the driver was understandable. He calmed the man by saying that he was not a part of the law enforcement agency. Nobody would come to know that his carriage had entered a prohibited zone. Then with the utmost politeness, he confided to this nondescript man his desired thought. The *tongawallah* lit another *bidi* and beckoned him to hop on to the carriage. Nudging the horse to move, he began: 'I do not remember anything about the inner fort. I will take you to an old Hakim Sahib. Once I had taken a lady patient there. Even that's a long time ago. If my memory is not at fault, I think she must have belonged to the place you are talking about.'

Soon they were standing near the *haveli* of the Hakim Sahib. Parking his carriage on one side, the *tongawallah* also followed him to the house. The *haveli* was old; passed on from forefathers to their children, and so on. The dispensary was large and gorgeous. The walls were decorated with pictures of ancient hakims. Hakim Sahib sat on an elevated seat. He was aged, fair-skinned; his eyes shone with the glint of experience. His persona exuded such an aura that one needed courage to pick up a conversation with him. He was examining the pulse of a patient. Looking at him together with the *tongawallah*, a smile danced down the lips of the Hakim Sahib as if he was enjoying the sight. When the crowd of patients thinned down a bit, he stated the reason for his appearance in the politest way. The reference to the inner fort made Hakim Sahib thoughtful. He closed his eyes as if trying to link up some lost chain of thoughts. He stared at him in wonder. The *tonga* driver stepped aside. After a while, Hakim Sahib opened his eyes. Then he said, 'Such faces lie buried deep below the earth…!'

'That means you know about the inner fort?' he asked with a note of optimism in his voice.

'Alas! Those unlucky denizens … all inmates of the inner fort went away… no one knows about their fate now. The river changed its course. Everything got buried in the sands of the desert. That, too, happened long ago. It is difficult to keep count of it.' His words were steeped in sorrow.

He asked sadly, 'Has the inner fort been buried in the river bed?'.

'This poor uninformed man has no information of what happened to people who lived in the inner fort. Nor about the havoc the two rivers played in their lives. Or, about their grief.

They were all men of integrity and never wanted others to know about their plight. The number of patients also dwindled because of it. A pious lady used to come here, depressed and sad. God only knows whether she is dead or alive. Alas! Alas!' Hakim Sahib's eyes became moist.

'Sir! I want to know the direction and the way to the place,' he said.

'There are two ways to go there,' he said. 'One is by the river and the second by the bridge. The journey via the bridge will be long and that by the river, short.'

In his heart of hearts, he selected the way across the river.

'You may go to the northern gate of the city. There is a *ghat* by the river. It is called the Meethe Shah *Ghat*. What its condition is now, God only knows. Go there and find out. Before leaving, please allow me to entertain you with tea. Ahmed Mian will bring tea for you.'

With these words, Hakim Sahib once again started examining his patients with total concentration.

He looked at the aged benevolent man with esteem. The state of his concentration and dedication must be a gift of God. A day will come, he thought, when man would pray for this kind of dedication and ask God to restore this lost legacy back to mankind.

Hakim Sahib had specified to him in detail the path to the inner fort. Now he had to proceed to the northern gate of the city. After having tea, he came out together with the *tongawallah*. Till now, he had not properly seen the *tonga*. It was an apology for a *tonga*. The wheels were out of shape, creaking as they moved along the way. The harness over the horse's head did not fit well. The footrest swung with the movement of the carriage. In short, everything was out of order. Now he felt scared of travelling in it. But also felt ashamed of such a thought. A little while ago, the carriage had come as a godsend when his hopes looked shattered. He shook off his thoughts and hopped on to the carriage. The *tonga* driver was busy tugging at his *bidi*. He looked fresh with the new piece of information. It was impossible to forget him after the manner in which the man had solved his problem. He decided to compensate the poor man to his satisfaction, no even more than his expectation. Within half an hour, they arrived at the northern gate. It would not go any further. No other vehicle plied till the Meethe Shah *Ghat*. He got off the carriage and gave him his due. The *tongawallah* expressed his regrets for not going further. He thanked the driver and proceeded to the Meethe Shah *Ghat* by descending the steps.

On the *ghat*, spread out on big trays, the vendors were selling *laddoo*s and *batasha*s. He came to know from them that the river had receded a lot. It happens during the months of May and June. The water of the river recedes, making the dry bed of the river appear broad and deep. People cross the river where the water remains shallow. A makeshift *ghat* was erected there where boatmen pick up passengers to ferry them to the other side. It took about 15 to 20 minutes to cross over. But now, the hurdle was the trudge on the sand. He had no experience of it and the heat was becoming unbearable. Coolies though, were available who carried passengers on their shoulders till the makeshift *ghat*. To escape the arduous task of walking on the sand, one had this other agonising thing on offer. He did not like it. As it was, he had only a small amount of luggage—a briefcase with papers, a pair of clothes, and a shaving kit. With these, there was no point in travelling on someone else's back. He thought it prudent to walk. There was a dam which had to be crossed first. To cross the Everest-like dam in the intolerable heat seemed a challenge, which he accepted. After all, a venture meant a challenge. Somehow, he managed to cross the hurdle of the dam but was soon out of breath. His courage seemed to sag, and his hopes were dashed to pieces. Trees that could provide shelter could not be seen. Of course, some Babul trees were there. He waited for a while to review his decision. He was on the verge of deciding to return when, far away, he saw a group of four people trudging along. It seemed that the group comprised of a man and three women. He admired their courage and felt ashamed of his lack of it. He then decided to trek along with them. They were walking at a faster pace. He tried to increase his pace. He might have taken one or two steps when his feet sank deep into the sand. He was unaware of the fact that one should not walk fast on sand, the path being unknown and treacherous. It was not an easy job, especially when the path was unknown. It brought to him the thoughts of the camels of the desert. Had he been an unrestrained ostrich, the journey would have been easier. The group had, by this time, proceeded further. The distance transformed them into shadow-like appearances. He slowly freed his feet off the sand and moved on. He was lucky the group stopped for a while. A seller of watermelons had made them tarry. He managed to make up the gap. He tramped slowly so as not to overtake them. Now he tried to look at the group from close quarters. There was an old man of 70 years or so. He was carrying a clock on his shoulders. An elderly lady with him seemed to be his wife. She was, now and then, helping him plod along, even bearing the burden of carrying the clock. Amongst the others, one seemed to be a middle-aged lady, while to ascertain the age of the other by her figure was difficult. She did not appear to be old enough. From a distance, she did not look like a teenager but was certainly young. A closer look could clear up things. His attempt now was to walk with the group. With this thought in mind, he tried to keep pace with it.

Now he was close to the group. The wind carrying millions of dust particles made it difficult to observe their faces. But their figures could be seen nevertheless. The man was advanced in age, and his wife, still stout and healthy. The man was still performing the duty of looking after his family. The middle-aged woman was plump and sexy. She seemed to be a bit careless with the handling of her sari. It was bordered, making her look attractive. She was not meant to be touched, best left to herself. Her eyes were large but sad. He was very close to them now. She saw him and looked surprised. Then she put the watermelon close to her chest and walked on. The act of hiding the watermelon amused him. But there she was, edging forward on the sand by the deft use of her heels. The youngest was adorned in a *salwar kameez*, wearing old-styled sandals. She stood on the threshold of adolescence, a passionate young girl. With age, she will also be like her partner walking by her side. It looked as if she had undertaken the journey under compulsion. Her face was beautiful but thoughtful. She also carried a watermelon. Sometimes while walking, she would place her hand on her mother's waist. The mother would remove it: 'Walk on your own,' she would quickly withdraw her hand and walk up straight. Then the girl would look like some object slithering on the sand. She looked conceited but sad. Maybe her name could be Mahelaqa, like the moon, he thought. But he had no right in passing comments on others. Others will always remain others. After all, he was only an agent of a realtor company; how can he understand others.

An agent that passed on to his customers whatever was told to him by the company, neither more nor less.

He again looked at the girl, from head to foot. No doubt, she was unmarried. When their eyes met, she felt embarrassed and adjusted her *dupatta*. The other lady remained unperturbed on such occasions; her body at ease, her steps confident. But her ease and confidence were like a magnet. Her appeal at times was capable of drawing one's self towards her completely without one being conscious of it; an unfelt kind of attraction. The mother and father were also moving with confident steps. The group's march on the sands took his memory far into the past. Each individual deserved an accolade for courage. Defying heat, dreary sand, and thirst, denying themselves the cool taste of the watermelon, they walked on. He tried to keep pace with them and succeeded. It came from the inspiration he picked up from the scene. Otherwise, he was not capable of such an act. He was helplessly pushing his body, driven by the desire for the fort which promised him a better future. He was possessed by dreams of this brighter future, the realisation of which lay in finding the inner fort. The managing director had handed him the key that could unlock this future.

Now he was walking together with the group consisting of four people. Some Babul trees were left behind, some stood in front. The old man would stare at him, turn away his eyes, and then stare back at him. Sometimes, their eyes met and then they would quickly avert them. They were on the verge of initiating a conversation when the *ghat* came into view. The boatmen were hollering for passengers to the inner fort. He had made up his mind to board the same boat in which these four would cross over. But bad luck was in store for him. A boatman came running along, snatched the clock from the old man's shoulders, took watermelons from both the women, and ran for his anchored boat close by. Either the boat belonged to the old man or he might have fixed the boat for the trip. He looked at their departure with desire-filled eyes. Suddenly the mother said, 'The poor man seems to be an outsider. Why not take him in.' The old man complied with the request and beckoned him to come over.

All of them were seated in the same boat. The boat left the shore, rocked a little, and then sailed steadily on the water. The wind was strong but not enough to make it difficult to use the oars. The boatman was a sturdy sailor. Here the boatmen are called sailors. The sailor took the responsibility of handling the big oar himself. He stood at the rear of the boat and started rowing. The young lady was looking at him through the corner of her eyes and blushing. An interesting game ensued. When the boat reached the middle of the river, the oars seemed to miss the target. The boatman passed an oar to the old man who was sitting in front, keeping a watch on the moving boat. The old man started using the oar from the opposite side. The boat picked up some speed.

He picked up a conversation with the young girl. She told him that she was returning after completing her Madhyamik examination. The centre of the examination was on this side of the river. They had to stay for a few days. So, all of them—father, mother, and sister-in-law—had come along with her. The sister-in-law took an interest in their conversation. She stared at him but soon averted her eyes to stare at the water. When he asked the girl whether her sister-in-law avoided talking, she replied that it was because married women were forbidden to talk to strangers. The boat soon rocked a bit and the watermelon with the sister-in-law rolled down towards his feet. He picked it up with both hands and handed it to the lady.

'It's a delicate fruit. Another fall and it would be reduced to smithereens.'

Bhabi placed it on her lap without a word. But her eyes gave away the unspoken words that entangled his own, that lay in between her lap and her bosom. The oars created murmurous sounds as the boat headed towards its destination.

The old man began to speak affectionately of the inner fort. He came to know that the family was a resident of the inner fort. The old man was not sure for how many generations they had been living there. The history of about 150 years or so was known to him. His father had been in the army. He was the commander of a platoon comprising of 60 constables. What majesty his father had! In sword-fighting, he was peerless. But the introduction of grenades and bombs had degraded the art of lancing. Now it has been reduced to showbiz. But he was happy nevertheless because, at least, he possessed one talent taught to him by his father. This new generation does not even know the art of swimming. Then suddenly the man became emotional. His eyes became moist.

'If we had not been bequeathed the land by our forefathers, God only knows where we would have been living!'

'What is the status of the inmates of the inner fort now? How can I meet them?'

The questions made all of them quiet. Despondency was writ large on their faces. The reaction to his questions worried him. The old man began to speak after a long interval of silence.

'The history of the inner fort is a long one,' he said. 'It has come to a stop, you can say.' The old man again paused in his narration. The speed of the boat became slow. The young girl pored over her question papers. Dulhan *Bhabi* was lost in the world of her thoughts. The oarsman was trying to find new ways of steering the boat against the flow of the river. The old lady was gaping into nothingness. Her husband looked towards her as if seeking her permission to begin again. The man began, probably because permission from his wife had been granted.

'It is called Inner Fort because it comprises of the leftover part of the main fort. Earlier it was called the "Diwani Fort"; spread out on a two-square-mile stretch. The inner plates inside the earth changed their positions, the river its course, and the Diwani Fort simply got submerged into the waters. But the inner part of the fort remained intact. Our family lived in the outer parts of the fort, possibly for centuries. The sinking of the fort made the family homeless. Bade Huzoor, the venerable elder, showed compassion for many inundated family members. My grandfather went over to live at the inner fort. From then, the part comprising of two rooms has saved us from being homeless. We are grateful to the owners of the inner fort and the elder son, Bade Babu, for his generosity. The family of the inner fort's owner is small. For the last three generations, no girl was born in the family. The family members have made the grandsons stay here since a long time. Bade Huzoor regretted the lack of girls in the family. He expected that one day a beautiful girl would be born, spread happiness in the house, grow up, throw tantrums, be naughty, take piggy rides on the backs of her brothers, pull their ears, and make faces. He, too, had no sisters. His wife came along, but she was no alternative to a daughter. Bade Huzoor bid farewell to this world with this regret in his heart. He left two sons behind. We call them Bade Babu and Chote Babu, for after the abolishment of the zamindari system, the titles of Bade Huzoor and Chote

Huzoor lost their relevance and are not used anymore. They are now referred to as Bade Babu and Chote Babu. Can this be a respectable way of addressing men of such high rank? Neither the majesty and splendour of the past remained nor the power and prestige. Everything vanished into thin air. Bade Babu had no offspring. I do not know what went wrong. Both the husband and wife were devoted to each other; a second marriage would have raised a hue and cry. Their mother, till she lived, tried all the means of rectification, superstition or otherwise. But nothing worked. The wife used to cry her heart out, many a time. With the passage of time, she was reduced to an embodiment of sorrow and regret. Chote Babu belonged to a different world altogether. There was a mystery about his persona. He had his education at Aligarh. God knows what he studied there! He remained pent up in his room. If he came out sometimes, he became the butt of all jokes. In this way, the ladies of the inner fort would get some amusement. The elder sister-in-law, especially, enjoyed this the most. To see her brother-in-law clad in a woman's garment was a cause for merriment. Sometimes the incessant laughter would bring tears to her eyes. But behind the laughter was hidden a deep sorrow, which neither time nor the inner fort could solve. Even though for a moment, with his effeminate gait and girlish bearing, Chote Babu at least provided some happiness for the Badi Dulhan.'

The agent had, by now, somewhat come to know about the inmates of the inner fort. It looked as if making a deal now would not be difficult. He was almost on cloud nine when the shout of the girl came to his ears.

'Dulhan *Bhabi* has fainted.'

The old lady was quick to catch hold of the collapsing woman. She placed her head on her lap and started fanning her. He soaked his handkerchief and poured drops of water on Dulhan *Bhabi*'s face and forehead.

Dulhan *Bhabi* opened her eyes; the tears from her eyes mixed with the water of the river and turned grey. She stared at the face of the stranger, but it looked hazy to her. Slowly things became clear to her, everything, the stranger, the sky, and the river.

'Nothing to worry about,' said the stranger, 'just acidity, nothing else. I will give you a Digene tablet. Chew it. It will ease your problem.'

'Must be so. Her whole body was affected by it,' the girl put a part of Dulhan *Bhabi*'s sari in place. It had dropped because of her sudden fall. He had watched the state of the woman when that part of her sari fell off. He did not know that a slight exposure of the body could set aflame his desire. The old man directed the oarsman to cautiously steer the boat. He looked calm now after the initial shock of the incident. The *ghat* was closer. He directed his look towards the old man as if expecting him to start the narration again. The experienced old man quickly read his thoughts.

'You are a traveller,' the old man began, 'your company is here for a short while. What will you do by listening to tales of sorrow? We, on the other hand, are patients of acidity. It can attack at any moment. We do not even carry medicines. It was good luck that you were ...'

'It happens sometimes,' he replied, 'not always. Look, now the lady seems to be at ease with herself.'

He looked at the old lady and the girl as if expecting them to nod. Both shook their heads in approval. But Dulhan *Bhabi* was abnormally calm. The old man began. 'If you will stay overnight at the inner fort, then we will narrate the rest of the story there...'

'I have to,' he quickly added.

He told them he had come to fix up a deal relating to the inner fort. His company was in talks with the archaeological department. He had an interest in ancient places and ruins and was a student of archaeology. A realtor firm had, after all, hired his services for the purchase of the inner fort.

The old man was taken aback with the information and asked, 'Will the inner fort be put up for sale?'

'The archaeological department does not want to develop it on its own. They want to sell it to some company and gain a direct profit,' he tried to explain.

'Will the inner fort be sold without taking the opinions of the inmates?'

'These are government issues that have to be settled between my company and the government.'

The information stunned them all. Even the oarsman was taken aback, as if someone had snatched away the oars from him. The fright brought the women almost on the verge of tears. Hardly had the oarsman come out of his shock when the river became turbulent. It rocked the boat, giving it a spin. To him, it seemed like the end of the road. The girl tried to comfort him.

'The boat won't go down. It happens.' She was right. The waves dashed against the sides of the boat and returned. He heaved a sigh of relief. He did not even know how to swim. The oarsman became active. He jumped and landed on the platform of the boat. Water had entered the boat because of the surge of the waves. The boat seemed to sink. The oarsman started throwing out the water with a container, while the old man took up the responsibility of steering the boat. When the water was cleared, the oarsman took up the oars from the old man. The boat was moving steadily. The girl asked him to come and sit in the middle of the boat to ward off his fear of falling into the river. He followed her advice.

Now *Bhabi* was sitting close to him. He had never seen such a sexy woman in his life. She must have been 35 or 36 years of age. Even in her silence, her body seemed to speak. He was in a fix about whether by changing his place, he had landed in a safe or risky zone. He was at the end of the third phase of his life, where one just performs what comes to mind. He was relishing the moment to the point of satiety. When the same old question was put to him, 'Will the inner fort be sold?' He looked around to find out who had asked the question. Everyone was tight-lipped. His sense of earlier satisfaction oozed out of him. He understood that the information had made the inmates of the boat speechless; their body language articulated grief, their lips were sealed with sorrow, eyes gazed into nothingness. It hurt them. He felt a sense of regret, akin to committing a sin. He was wallowing in between them both. But he was not at fault. The government policy was to be blamed. In this remote area, there was neither a Medha Patkar nor an Arundhati Roy. Who will be able to protest? The oarsman broke in, 'We will put up a fight. As the boat does not move without our wish, the policy of the government too will not.' The words inspired the inmates of the inner fort, putting life into them. The old man said, 'The poor man should not be blamed. He is an employee, a slave, bound to carry out orders given to him. Let him follow the orders. We were refugees from the day when calamity struck for the first time. The second time, it was the Partition, and the third now is the policy of the government. The policy does not take us into consideration. It is implemented and we bow to it.'

But the excited oarsman could not accept the unacceptable policy. 'We ply boats. We know what kind of policy we need.'

The old man understood and appreciated the sentiments of the young oarsman.

'Law has no place for sentiments,' he tried to explain to him. 'Now boy, throw the anchor aside. We are tired, even our co-passenger too. He is our guest. We have to complete our duty of being true hosts. We will deal with the men when they come to talk to us. You have been performing the duty of an oarsman since childhood, though I have made the boats for you.'

'Yes, Dada,' he replied. 'The land is close. You can see the spires of the inner fort.'

The words were inspiring like the emotional and courageous speech of the captain to the mates of a sinking ship. He was thinking about the success of his mission. He should not have told them that the inner fort may be sold. Even if the survey was accepted, the completion of the project would take years. It was unwise of him to create tension at this point in time. The hunter does not give notice to the birds when he is out to destroy their nests. The hunter does it all of a sudden. The destroyers do not follow the rules of advance information.

'They say that 10 to 12 rooms of the inner fort were burnt down because of firecrackers?' He sought another piece of information.

They remained silent as if burning with the rage of fires.

The boat slowly edged towards the land.

'Even the guest house of the inner fort was reduced to ashes,' the old man broke in. 'If you agree, you may stay at our modest dwelling. The girls would arrange things for you. Insha Allah, you will not face any problem.'

He was tired. He dozed off immediately but felt someone pass by his room to enter the next one. He would not have woken had he not heard the *chun, chun* sound of jewellery worn on a woman's feet. The soft movement of feet, and the sound of jewellery was music to his ears. He fell asleep again. He woke up to find the old man walking towards the masjid. Possibly it was time for *maghrib*, the evening prayer. He sat up. His neighbours were preparing to light lanterns and other sources of light. The chimneys of lanterns and lamps were being cleaned. The supply of electricity was poor. If the supply sometimes was restored, the prevalence of low voltage did not solve the problem.

He was badly in need of a cup of tea. He thought of calling someone. But before he did that, the young girl who had taken the Madhyamik exam stood with a steaming cup of tea. There was that heart-winning smile on her lips as if giving him greetings. Together with the cup, it seemed that she had bequeathed to him the whole world. Before sipping, he cast his grateful eyes towards her.

'Sugar, okay?' She asked. With the reply coming in the affirmative, she walked softly towards the door and vanished behind the hanging curtain.

Unknowingly, he had discovered a totally new world. Even after his information, such a decent treatment! Before he finished the last sip, the girl appeared again on the scene.

'More tea!' She enquired.

'No, thanks,' he replied and handed her both the cup and saucer.

Their fingers touched and eyes met and it created a turbulence of sorts. Though he had studied in a co-educational institution, and had come across similar moments, the effect was never like this. It was a different world; unusual things, new sensations. Now it dawned upon him that in pursuit of material goods, he had wasted the best part of his life. The 'dream project' had woven a web around him. The coal business simply blackens one's hands, but this land business ... His excitement made him tremble. He managed to overcome the feeling with some effort. What goes out, has to be brought in. That is what has to be done.

He directed his attention towards the deal in order to change the focus of his thoughts. He brought out the relevant papers from his briefcase, but the low voltage made him incapable of perusing the words. He waited patiently for the voltage to increase. The decision about the plan had to be taken today. He proceeded towards the door so as to call someone for some alternative arrangement.

The curtain lifted and someone with a delicate air of femininity, the index finger on the chin, walked past, the jewellery on the feet creating a *chun, chun* sound.

He was shocked; the sudden appearance and ghost-like disappearance made him gape in wonder. The voltage dimmed further, plunging the place into darkness. He was incapable of thought; he froze. He came to his senses when a dim light appeared before him. A henna-marked hand was holding an emergency lamp aloft. The verandah now seemed to be bathed in light. He tried to look at the face behind the curtain but failed in his attempt. The hand placed the lamp and vanished. He tried to locate the identity of the person and came to the conclusion that it must be the same woman who was not permitted to talk in front of strangers.

'Can she be the widow?' He thought.

He remembered an eight-year-old boy running towards the *Bhabi* when they had arrived at the inner fort. Her attractive body had become active. She had bent over the boy and kissed him on the forehead before proceeding towards the room. Apart from the old man, he had not seen any male member in the household. Then he remembered the strange figure that had walked with the *chun, chun* sound past him. It was an enigma. He failed to solve the puzzle.

He soon got lost in the official papers. The 'dream project' of the inner fort was erected on the debris of possibilities. His company was said to be a leader among visionary groups; their visions of the future were an asset, like the East India Company. As soon as the company came to know that at the north gate of Bahadurabad, a bridge over the Meethe Shah *Ghat* was being considered, it took upon itself the responsibility of discovering the inner fort. Experts opined that it would be a bad investment. But the elderly lady in charge refused to listen to them. The utmost loss, according to her, could be the expenses incurred on the pilot survey. Her company ran on the realm of possibilities. Thus, he was deputed on this project without worrying about the losses that it would incur. He had to perform his duty. He scanned the list of directions that had to be followed. The topmost was the survey of the location, value, and worth of the properties of the inner fort. Secondly, the archaeological value of the structure and ruins of the inner fort. The worth of the fort, as far as tourism was concerned, also had to be explored. Could the inner fort be considered a national heritage site? If so, then the company may be granted government concessions on this count. He would play a key role in helping the company reap benefits in the development of the site. He may, as well, become a figure of national pride. He soon got lost in a different world. The new experiments of life and new sensations seemed to lose their meaning.

Watermelons, cups of tea, emergency lamps, the jewellery worn on feet, and the sound of music created by it, boat, oars, all seemed to belong to the world of imagination, not the stuff of the real world. He got immersed in his dream project to such an extent that he hardly noticed the entry or the departure of the young girl when she came with the second cup of tea. He came to his senses when she was arranging the food for dinner. First, she spread out the mat on the floor, and then placed a tablecloth on it. There was no provision for a dinner table, for there was none. After placing the food on the tablecloth, she called for her father. The old man soon appeared on the scene. With the increase in the voltage, things eased a bit; otherwise, the heat was becoming intolerable.

'The inner fort contained 72 rooms,' the old man began during dinner, 'divided into 12 units, each having its own courtyard, verandah, open space and in the midst, a durbar-styled hall with verandahs on all sides. All the rooms around the hall were under Bade Babu and Chote Babu. One of the rooms served as the office, while another, the bigger one, as the storeroom. The others were meant for residence and for the purpose of ornamentation. All the courtyards were decorated with trees bearing different kinds of fruits; lemons, custard apples, white mulberries, mangoes, and guavas. The niches of the house were decorated with dodder plants; it was full of life. But after the death of Bade Huzoor, the place became deserted.

Be it the gems, stones, gold, silver, wealth, land, offspring, all lost their sheen. The greatest crisis facing the family was the decreasing number of children; only two survived. Bade Babu had no successor and Chote Babu was of a weird nature. Whatever verve existed in the family was because of the servants.

'The storeroom was full of family inheritances descended from the forefathers. Sometimes they used to call it the family museum. Bows and arrows, swords and shields, armoury, brass, copper, silverware, ancient styled dressing table, mirror stands, bric-a-brac, and gallery of expensive garments were found to be plentiful. Innumerable kinds of brocade and embroidery filled the gallery. Short-sleeved bodice, blouse, skirt, coat, *angarkhas*, and *sherwanis* were aplenty. Most of their names were difficult to pronounce. It can be said that the place was a treasure house of women's dresses passed down the ages as gifts from different rulers; some were also purchased according to the tastes of the time. But with the passage of time, all these expensive clothes became a part of the storeroom and nothing else. The outfits inside the boxes were centuries old, especially the *benarasi* costumes, which now have gone out of fashion. Bade Babu was not interested in the family household goods or knick-knacks. Of course, every year, he would personally supervise the cleaning and dusting of them. Nowadays, special servants cannot be found who were considered experts in the handling of these items. So, they had to take the help of different agencies to look after these expensive items. Chote Babu, on the other hand, was enamoured of them. He would throw tantrums for the keys to the rooms which were under the custody of the Badi Dulhan. He would force her to open the doors of the storeroom and remain pent up inside the whole day. When he came out, he would be covered with dust all over him. But there would be a smile of victory on his face. Badi Dulhan would tease him: "Brother tell me whether you remain in the store or bridal room. Once inside, you don't want to come out. I will conduct a raid one day."

Though it was said in jest, he looked worried. "Don't you do that *Bhabi*. Allah will be displeased with me," he pleaded before her.

"*Bhabi* will be displeased, not Allah, if she catches you. There is the mirror from Belgium, which she does not want anyone to touch. She has plans to gift the dressing table to your bride."

'The dressing table was actually a gift to Bade Babu's grandmother from the English Sub-Divisional Officer. He held grandmother in the highest esteem and was also inclined towards her. Grandmother could ride a bicycle and also knew how to drive. Bade Babu's grandfather had won a motor car at a horse race in Poona. She had fallen in love with grandfather's skill at horse riding. Grandmother's mother was a broad-minded lady. All her life, she courted the laboratory assistant of Prabhat Studio and though unwed, gave birth to a child who happened to be the future grandmother of Bade Babu. It is said that once she also came here but returned without success. It is said that the Chote Dadi (Bade Babu's grandmother) once went alone to participate in horse racing in Calcutta but did not return to the inner fort again. She had gone there alone. It was possible that she might have been killed in the Direct Action Riots of 1946 on her return journey on the train. With her death, came to end a bright chapter in the history of the inner fort.'

'Decline set at the inner fort with the death of Choti Dadi. Independence in 1947, Partition, and after the establishment of Pakistan, one could sense the start of decay of the inner fort.'

'I fail to understand,' he said.

'I'll tell you all,' the old man said. 'Respected Grandfather's fault was that he decided not to opt for Pakistan. Then started the attempts from all quarters to drive away the inmates of the inner fort: government, political parties, jealous neighbours, all tried their best. Grandfather was even branded a Pakistani and put behind bars. They even tried to grab the property, making use of the Enemy Property law. Grandfather and father fought legal battles; did not give in to threats. Grandmother had known Bidhan Babu[1] even before the Partition of the country.

1 Bidhan Chandra Roy was the first chief minister of West Bengal.

The old association with him came in handy and his requests worked. Grandfather's dream of dying and his body being interred in the motherland came to pass. The zamindari was abolished, the workers issued the receipt of land and grandfather breathed his last. Grandmother had also died, followed by Bade Babu's father. They all went one after the other. The inner fort became an image of abandonment. Bade Babu, though young, was forced to marry. Badi Dulhan took up the reins of the household.'

Bhabi entered at this point and started collecting the utensils from the spread-out tablecloth. She did so, quietly, with bated breath. The young girl might have fallen asleep. One part of *Bhabi*'s sari was slipping away as she went about with her work. Her body and age were not enough to make her hold herself together. Somehow, she managed to collect the dishes and went out of the room. To him, she looked like a deer. She came inside the room like a sprinter and then vanished into thin air. His eyes looked surprised and his heart skipped a beat. The old man began the tale again.

'After the entry of the Badi Dulhan, joviality returned to some extent at the inner fort. But not the kind of life and gaiety associated with Ghalib; just a little bit. If there was laughter, it lacked merriment; music without sound, things were devoid of jauntiness. It was something in between life and death.'

The old man's eyes became wet, but he kept on with the tale. 'Badi Dulhan waited for the arrival of a child. But it seemed the wait became longer and longer till seven years had passed.'

'Maybe it was the wish of the Almighty,' he said in a tone of solace.

The old man went on unperturbed. 'The hopes of the inmates of the inner fort were slowly dashed to pieces. Ammi Bi even used superstitious methods. Hakim Haziq, the best physician on the other side of the Ganga, failed in his attempts, though he used all his skill and means as far as knowledge of medicine was concerned. Success evaded him. Dulhan *Bhabi* remained childless. There was not even a flicker of hope. After a few months, another soul departed from the fort; Ammi Bi died without seeing the face of her grandchild. Amongst the bereaved members of the family remained the two sons and Badi Dulhan, who was childless.'

The old man heaved a deep sigh.

'Why didn't Ammi Bi arrange the marriage of Chote Babu?' he asked.

For a moment, the old man stammered, unable to come up with an answer. He soon controlled himself and said, 'A little while ago, you must have seen someone wearing earrings, ornaments on the wrists and feet coming towards my room, and then return.'

'Who was she?' he enquired.

'That was Chote Babu.'

He was baffled.

'Far away from his own identity: in love with effeminacy, walk, gait, mannerism, all like a woman. It's good he does not come out of the house; otherwise, the youths of the area would have played havoc with him. His rounds are limited to the boundaries of the house and the area of the tenants, till the rooms of this poor man. Apart from the stretch of a gully, ours is the first house that he has to negotiate. More or less, you can say, he moves around in purdah.'

'Interesting,' he laughed.

'Maybe for you,' the old man replied. 'For us, this is an open secret. It is not play-acting. It must have been years,' he stopped, tried to reminiscence, and recapture the past. He began again, 'Both the brothers were young at that time. Bade Babu was a bit older, but Chote Babu must have been three or four years of age. Both of them were the apple of the eye of Choti Dadi; incomplete without each other. At such a tender age, Choti Dadi left. After the mishap, Chote Babu became quiet. Sometimes in moments of frenzy, he would enter Choti Dadi's bedroom, climb naked on the table, mock fight with his own image in the mirror, and ask her to return. In the absence of a reply from her, he would throw blows at the mirror. The Belgian mirror would not break but Chote Babu's hands would get bruised. Many a time, Badi Dadi would catch hold of him and bring him back to his mother. "Hold this naked devil of yours," she would say, "at least tie a black thread on his waist. This way, he may be safe from bad spirits." The mother would smack him many a times. He would cry till sleep overpowered him. Chote Babu had developed such attitudes; nothing could be done about them.'

'If that was the case, why was he not taken to a psychiatrist?'

The old man smiled.

'We do not know such a doctor exists. Of course, Badi Dadi used to take him to a renowned hakim on the other side of the river. There was no lack of treatment on that count. But the state of Chote Babu's health did not change. He would open the wardrobe of Choti Dadi, spread out the *benarasi* saris and other dresses on the floor. Then he would roll on them. The embroidery works on the saris would pierce his body and make him bleed. The precious white stones of the floor would turn red with his blood. Sometimes, he would be dragged out of the room in an unconscious state. As a result of this, all items of Choti Dadi were transferred to the storeroom and her room was locked.'

The story had hardly reached this point when *Bhabi* once again entered the room, balancing the extended part of her sari with her hand.

'If you have finished your conversation, can I please take away the mat? It's late in the night. Rumi has fallen asleep. Munni too dozed off.'

The old man looked towards him and saw signs of curiosity on his face.

He said, 'It would be over in ten minutes.'

'Accha,' said *Bhabi*, and left the room.

The story went on uninterrupted.

'Chote Babu remained gloomy for a long time. Sometimes he would lie near the threshold of Choti Dadi's house, at others, bang at the lock of the locked storeroom. He would be beaten many a time but to no avail. Ammi Bi left him to his state. When he grew up, they sent him to a boarding school at Aligarh for higher studies. It was during his stay at Aligarh that Ammi died. When he returned, the state of frenzy increased, for the last source of love and affection was also gone. His condition deteriorated to such an extent that they quickly sent him back to Aligarh. He managed to complete his studies there. He wrote a treatise on archaeology that became the subject of acclamation. But he failed to come out of his state of fixation. After his return from Aligarh, he refused to come out of the inner fort. He built such a web around himself that even the well-conversant failed to penetrate it. Sometimes when he opened up, he would try to convince himself that his disguise was the reality. Disguise was appearance. As a proof, he would reply: "Logs of wood dare to challenge the waves only when their state changes into the shape of a boat." He was searching for new forms in the milling crowd. He wanted to be of some use to the whole of mankind. In the world of a thousand colours, he found one successful way out, and that was to be above the real. But in such an attempt, he was considered to be so strange that his presence on this earth itself became in doubt. So why shouldn't one touch him to make him understand that he was still living? Why did no one do so? Instead, they try to stop him from his act which he naturally didn't like. There was no one to stop him anyway.

'The keys of all the rooms were with Badi Dulhan. One day he managed to get hold of the keys of the storeroom despite opposition from Bade Babu. Getting possession of the keys was like reaching the stars. He went inside, opened the gallery of knick-knacks and selected dresses according to his choice: He adorned himself with Rajasthani *ghagra choli, qamarband* with designs, *tika*, bangles, ornaments of the ears, a nose pin, and flower-decked garments. He wore all kinds of bangles that went up to his wrists. His ears and nose were not pierced but the madness made him force down the pins into them, making them bleed. Blood oozed out and lay on his hands; he rubbed it on his lips, which instantly turned red. Then he stood before the Belgian mirror. He stood there looking at himself; his lips smiling. The image of Choti Dadi swam before him. Jaws, eyes, shoulders, palms, waist, knees, heels, feet; all open-eyed, clear. He danced with joy. He caught his image in the mirror with both hands and pressed so tight that the dressing table on which he stood shook, making him lose balance and fall together with the mirror on the ground. The *ghagra* from the knees came up to his waist, the *choli* tore, bangles broke, and the earrings fell off. The Belgian mirror had the mark of his lips, and a thin line of blood ran from his thighs to the right knees. Chote Babu lay unconscious and flat on the ground. It was a bizarre scene. The crashing sound made both Badi Dulhan and Gulshan Dai rush to the spot. The door was forced open, the situation was gauged and Gulshan Dai was quickly dispatched towards the male household.

'"Your Chote Babu has created a scene. He is lying unconscious, half naked, with a female dress on his body. God only knows the reason behind this mystery!"

'The servants brought him to his room, adjacent to the male household, after resettling his clothes on his body. After the death of Bade Huzoor, Bade Babu had never even waved a finger at his brother. But today, he was bursting with anger. The dressing table's English mirror had been severely dented. The act could not go unpunished. When Chote Babu came to his senses, he was asked to appear in the corner room. Then without a question, Bade Babu started beating him with a cane. Chote Babu neither screamed nor wept. There was neither protest nor prayer for clemency. He bore the punishment with such forbearance that Bade Babu was reduced to tears. He picked up Chote Babu from the floor and embraced him crying inconsolably. Badi Dulhan was impatiently walking to and fro outside the door. She heard the sounds of weeping and could not control her feelings. She forcibly opened the door and sneaked in. Finding Badi Dulhan face-to-face was enough to make both of them break into tears. It was a grief-stricken moment that happens only with kindred in moments of pain. She helped both wash their faces and offered mulberry sherbet. For the first time, both of them understood how sweet the taste of mulberry could be, picked from their own garden. After partaking the sherbet, both remained quiet for a long time.

'With the sound of the *maghrib azaan*, Bade Babu walked for *namaaz* with guilty steps. Badi Dulhan used affectionate words of reprimand to Chote Babu: "Chi! You should not have done that!"'

The old man stopped his narration. He tried to find some meaning into the bizarre activities of Chote Babu. What was this man of 25 or 26 years of age trying to prove to his brother, Badi Dulhan, and well-wishers? What was the message conveyed through his body language? It was a mystery. All parts of his body were intact, healthy, what more? What was the need of the mirror before him? To see his own self? It needed no clarification. Was he trying to disguise himself by taking on female costumes? That, too, in the most bizarre way possible! But being in disguise was not painful; rather, it added colour to life. It was a preface of the inner self, the accomplishment of desire. If it contained something more, then maybe it was beyond his understanding. For a long time, he was caught in the web of such complex thoughts. Then he blinked. The old man saw his state and continued with his story.

'This is why Chote Babu's marriage did not take place. The whole community came to know of it. Families of his class stopped sending marriage proposals. This crisis of the inner fort was unimaginable.'

'This was a cruel, one-sided decision against Chote Babu. Anyway, please carry on,' he pleaded to the old man.

'It's late in the night. We will meet in the morning after the morning *namaaz*. You are not a late riser, I suppose?' the old man enquired.

'Not at all,' he said. 'If required, I can stay up for the whole night and yet get up early. I am a professional.'

It was not clear whether the old man understood him or not. He got up and said, 'Good night. We will meet tomorrow in the morning.'

'Good night.'

The old man left the story incomplete and went out of the room. Lights from most of the windows had been extinguished. However, there was light still coming from one of the windows.

A shadow also seemed to move behind its curtain. It might have been five minutes or more after the departure of the old man when the curtain from his door slightly moved. *Bhabi* came inside the room once again. She tried to collect the spread-out mat from the floor. He lay facing towards the mat, his hands dangling. She was sitting on her haunches. Unknowingly, his hands brushed some parts of her body. He looked into her half-closed eyes. They were like an oasis in a desert. She seemed to be caught in between the dilemma of saying or not saying it. Finally, she managed to say, 'May I bring *paan* for you?'

'Usually, I don't take it. But I do not avoid it also.'

'Hospitality, for us, without *paan* is incomplete,' she said. 'With or without tobacco?' She asked.

He did not reply, just shook his head. He left it for her to decide. She folded the mat and went out. To fall asleep now was out of the question. Intimacy, then craving, then this feeling of being surrounded by darkness; of walls on all sides. In such an eerie silence, you hear the sounds of crickets. He listened to the sounds, for there was nothing else to do. He soon picked up the sound of footsteps near the threshold. She came up with the *paan*. But it was only one piece of *paan* and that spoke of the destitute condition of the family. She extended her hand from one end of the camp cot and said, '*Paan* for you!'

"Thanks,' he said and stood up.

'Look up!'

He did, and with that she shoved the *paan* inside his mouth. Then she handed him cloves and cardamom.

This momentary intimacy was enough to drive him crazy. It was as if he was losing his senses. He tried to control his feelings. While leaving the room, she turned back and said, 'Mosquitoes are everywhere today. Let me bring you a Tortoise-brand mosquito coil,' she went out of the room. But this time, she took a long time to return. Now sleep was far away from his thoughts. It must have been midnight. He was losing hope, but could still see light at the window. A shadow could be seen moving to and fro near the window curtain. His eyes were glued to the window. He gave up hope when the window light was switched off and the shadow behind the curtain vanished. The silence all around deepened. The lamp post in the lane, ashamed of its dim light, stood there without casting a shadow underneath itself. He tried to sleep, but before he could, the sounds of footsteps were heard near the door. He looked around and saw that the curtain was lifted. She moved towards him with soft feline steps. It seemed that she had adorned herself afresh with *ghagra, chunni, qamarband*, and ornaments on the ankles. She had her *ghagra* lifted up to her knees. Her calf was broad like a palm tree, and burnished with the glitter of the *ghagra* embroidery. She came close to him and stopped to take a breath. For him, it was like a surge of waves in the sea.

'Where's the Tortoise coil?' he asked in alarm.

'Up there in the storeroom,' she said.

'Storeroom?'

'Yes, up there. Come with me to the storeroom. You can get fresh air and bring something from there too.'

She dragged him from the camp cot. Both walked towards the storeroom. It seemed as if the lamp post had snuffed out its light. It was a bright moonlit night. Both of them walked behind each other like shadows towards the inner room of the fort. When they arrived at the storeroom, she took out the keys, opened it and both got lost inside.

After the morning prayer, the old man came inside the room at the appointed hour. He saw both the mosquito coils reduced to embers, the stands standing still. He lay on the camp cot face down, leg spread out awkwardly. It showed that he was still fast asleep. The old man did not wake him up and went out of the room.

The bell of the madrasah rang at seven and he woke up with the sound. The old man was standing in the verandah, whispering something to himself. Maybe he was reciting the *darood* or some *ayaat*s from the Quran. He got up from the camp cot and walked towards the old man. He wished him and both exchanged pleasantries.

'How did you pass the night, young man?'

'The Tortoise coil helped. I slept peacefully.'

'That is what we do when mosquitoes play havoc.'

'It worked wonders. What about the rest of the tale? I would like to hear it.'

'Not much is left. I could have completed it last night. But we were all tired after the walk on the sands.'

'You are right. From the desert, if you arrive at the oasis, it allays the pain.'

'Oasis? But here there are only thorns…'

'Your home is like an oasis for me,' he said. 'Otherwise, I would have been wandering in the wild in this unknown part of the town.'

The old man looked at him with affectionate eyes and then began the tale.

'That day when Bade Babu beat up his younger brother, he spent the day pacing about agitatedly. Badi Dulhan tried her best to make him forget the unfortunate incident. If the elder had taken action against the mistake of the younger, she told him, it was only expected. It was not something that had to be taken to heart. But Bade Babu's torment kept on increasing. In the meantime, Chote Babu entered the storeroom four or five times and yet Bade Babu did not say a word. Rather, he tried to avoid it when he came to know about it. Now Bade Babu's only worry was about finding a good marriage proposal for his brother. A good life partner was capable of leading him away from his bizarre activities. But Chote Babu had been turned into a prisoner of his own weird acts. In such a situation, who would be ready to risk their life with him? Chote Babu would be in his elements in the storeroom, but outside he moved like a wet cat.

'One day, Badi Dulhan was in a mood to tease him. When he politely asked for the keys of the room, Badi Dulhan refused. He started throwing tantrums like a kid.

"Have you forgotten the day's punishment?" She asked. "It's your luck that your brother does not come along this way. Otherwise, he would have peeled off your skin this time."

"Bhaiyya becomes angry for no reason," he replied. "Instead, he should pat me on my back. Do you not know what I have achieved? I have achieved victory like Akbar the Great. No, even greater than him. Like Ashoka the Great—dressed in the knick-knacks of the storeroom I arrive at the battlefield. These ornaments and dresses are my weapons. I become the victor of both the worlds. That is the time when I am transformed into a complete whole. I achieve something substantial."

'Badi Dulhan laughed wholeheartedly at his nonsensical idea.

'This enraged him and he said: "You don't believe me. You want the proof. Come to the storeroom quietly when I call you."

"Okay," she replied. "I will be there."

'He took the keys and walked into the storeroom with élan. Badi Dulhan waited for the call. It came after an hour. She was caught in a fix. She was vacillating but had accepted the challenge from her brother-in-law. She could not back out now. It was noon and she slowly trudged towards the room. With a palpitating heart, she entered the room. The scene inside was enchanting. He shone like a bright star in the firmament. He was not gazing into the mirror. This time he was looking towards Badi Dulhan. She was being drawn towards him by some unknown mysterious force. From the gallery of knick-knacks, it seemed that someone was addressing her. Though the sound was emanating from the gallery, when she stared at his red ruby-like lips, they seemed to be lisping. The words from the gallery were getting submerged and losing themselves amongst the movement of his lips.

"With the arrival of evening, you desire to give yourself up completely. This intoxication helps you lose yourself. You feel scared too. The fear of losing yourself makes you plant your lips on my shoulders. Then like the squirrel, you feel safe, leading you to the world of intricate dreams. No safe resting place can be found better than this. Sometimes it can be transformed into a dark cave with no doors or windows. Then you will not be a part of the cave but will be transformed into a cave yourself."

'Encircled in the midst of the echoing words, *Bhabi* was being mysteriously attracted towards them. The burnished lips of Chote Babu were drawing *Bhabi*'s lips towards his self. She did not walk; her body was being drawn towards another body.

With the intention of getting merged into the other, she asked the question: "Who are you?"

"Whoever it may be!" came the reply.

'She is drawn further. "I am entering into you. Open your door. Come into this resting place. You have lived your life for this."'

'This time, what was within the embrace of Chote Babu, was not the Belgian mirror. It was Badi Dulhan. Since then, whenever he asked for the keys, Badi Dulhan willingly parted with them and waited for his call.

'A piece of good news was doing the rounds in the precincts of the inner fort. This was related to Badi Dulhan. Bade Babu had arranged to enlighten all the denizens of the place about it with a celebration. The occasion was being celebrated with pomp and gaiety. But soon, a fire broke out in the storeroom. The fire engulfed not only the storeroom but reduced 12 rooms of the inner fort into ashes. Chote Babu somehow managed to bring out Badi Dulhan out of the fire. Possibly, Bade Babu perished in the fire. No trace of him was ever found after that. Badi Dulhan never set her foot in that space ever, though Chote Babu repaired two rooms and they were made habitable once again.'

'What made Badi Dulhan do that?' He asked in surprise.

'I do not have the answer. I cannot tell you. Why don't you ask her yourself?'

'But where is she? Any idea?'

'You have met her. She came with us on the boat. She served food, gave you *paan*, arranged Tortoise coil and then … Badi Dulhan lives here, with me …'

He looked bewildered. The dream-like tour of the inner fort with her in her attractive dress, the star-studded storeroom, innumerable coloured lights, mulberry sherbet, those dreamy eyes … intoxicating state … What do they all mean? He looked shaken. Then he saw last evening, the eight-year-old boy standing before him with the tea kettle.

'Ammi has sent this for you. She is having a bad headache since last night. She could not sleep. She told me to apologise to you for being late.'

'You,' he stammered. 'Are you her son?'

The old man smiled. 'Yes, he is the only son of Badi Dulhan.'

Far away in the distance he could hear the *chun, chun* sounds from the footsteps of someone trudging along. Not Chote Babu, it was rather the Chote Piya of Badi Dulhan, who was on his way. He thought about him in this new light.

He quickly emptied the cup. He caressed the child, tapping his cheeks. The child looked at him with expectant eyes as if looking for a confidant in him. But hearing the footsteps of Chote Piya coming closer, he felt his own steps were receding. He felt that between the both of them, the little kid and Chote

Piya, he had become an extra. He quickly dressed up, collected his belongings, and headed towards the river.

At the *ghat*, the boatman was shouting out for one passenger only. Last passenger for the boat.

The elderly managing director was seated in her chamber, perusing the file 'Inner Fort Project'. It was a brief report. 'The said location consists only of debris and water. Fascinating sights where boatmen search for unknown objects. This worthless man was not fit to be a part of the project. He is ashamed of his worthlessness. Apologies.'

After reading the report, the old lady felt perturbed. Then her eyes became wet.

THE STOPPED CLOCK

SIDDIQUE ALAM

The hands of the clock had stopped permanently at 13 past two and two seconds. Sitting on the bench under the shed, I am trying to understand the oval dial of the clock, the roman letters of which had become dimmed and its edges covered with spider webs. I wonder when the clock might have stopped. I am 35 years old. Is there apparently any difference between us? Just like the clock, I have also stopped for a while because there was no announcement about the arrival of my train, its departure time being four hours ago.

I am trying to survey the place with wide open eyes.

It is a usual day and an ordinary station that we are accustomed to see.

I have bid farewell to the city of my birth. I am leaving the city like a failure. But it seems after relinquishing me, the city, with a feeling of guilt, now wants to take me back. Its first step in this direction is to delay my train for an indefinite amount of time.

Despite being in the midst of a city, a station is free from its clutches. I am enjoying that freedom with a one-way ticket in my pocket. A bit of patience, I tell myself, and I would be far away. Nobody can stop me, neither by erecting obstacles in the way of the railway tracks nor by stopping the hands of the clock. Maybe I am a loser, but the journey of my life is yet to end. I am only 35 years old. I have to go far away from this place. The most important thing is that I am satisfied that the address I am carrying in my pocket is not my last destination. It is a temporary waiting place that can help me make a new beginning. After all man is born free. The sun does not select a particular spot to shine, nor is every wave that dashes against the shore the last one, losing which the boatman would have to wait all his life for another wave.

An old coolie, wringing *khaini* in the palms of his hands, passes by me. He is clad in a white *banian* and dhoti, his red flannel shirt thrown on his left shoulder.

'Since when has the clock stopped?' My question stops him in his stride. He turns around, his tired, thoughtful eyes staring at me. A sense of shame overpowers me. He may be an illiterate coolie, not a station employee who is answerable for such a question. 'I am sorry,' I quickly add, 'I should not have put the question to you. I take back my words.'

'Why sir?' he stands by the side of the bench, and looks at me with a sense of intimacy. 'People will be asking questions about a stopped clock, isn't it? They cannot to be blamed. The story of the stopped clock is well known but only the signal man

Gocharan Ray has the right to tell its tale. He had spent all his life showing green and red flags to trains and has retired today.'

'Who has replaced him?' my question betrays my foolishness. My imprudence had always entangled me in thoughtless acts.

'Why don't you ask the station master?' The coolie moves away. 'It's a question that requires an answer; otherwise, you will regret it all your life.'

I was not ready for such an unexpected turn of events. I thought that my relationship with the city had been cut off forever. What do I make of a station that has ignored me, as if the ticket in my pocket is of no worth? Once again, I look at the dial of the clock hanging from the shed. It had stopped at 13 past two and two seconds. What might have happened when it stopped? Did an accident take place at the station? Had any incident of murder taken place? Was it at the time of the departure or arrival of an important leader? An attack by Naxalites? Or was the place the site of a communal incident?

The coolie returned again. This time he was wearing his shirt. 'Unless you hear the story,' he says, 'your train will not arrive. This is the rule here. It may take weeks, months, or even years and you have to move from one platform to another with your suitcase. Once, a passenger alighted here to board another train. He faced a similar dilemma. He asked the same question about the clock but I do not know what happened and why he refused to listen to the story. Do you know what happened to him?'

'How can I?' I replied impatiently. 'The city hardly gave me any time so that I could listen to stories.'

'You are becoming irritated unnecessarily, Sir,' he said. 'I want to tell you about the man. The fact is nobody knows much about him. Some say he went to the city and did not return. Others say he took another train that never reached its destination. Some may even tell you that a prostitute took him to her house by the railway tracks where he developed leprosy and is slowly dying there. There is also no dearth of people who say he is still moving, suitcase in hand, amidst platforms, difficult to spot in the teeming crowd of passengers.'

'You mean to say he can be anyone, even me?'

'Did I say that, sir?' He was on the verge of leaving. 'It seems you have tasted bitter gourd.'

I was staring at the departing coolie's back. The constant use of the flannel shirt had not only exposed its fibres, it had also thinned the material exposing the bones of the man's neck. I have no hesitation in saying that I did not believe him. Since the time when suitcases developed wheels, the number of coolies has dwindled in stations. The last nail was the introduction of the backpack. Either passengers drag their suitcases on wheels, or carry luggage in their backpacks, leaving the coolies with little work. So, this may be their way of passing time. But why am I here sitting with my suitcase thinking that the delay of my train may be of significance? A train's non-arrival carries no meaning in the hustle and bustle of man's life, unless it chugs along to arrive at the station with all its smoke and stink.

I take a deep breath. Now that the matter seems to have become complicated and I am involved in it, there is no option but to enquire with the station master about the arrival of my train. After all, what makes the man so busy that supposing he loses sight of his work, will all the trains dash against each other running on the tracks, even the ones yet to come out of the factory?

The station master's office was three steps down the platform, its thick walls a sign of the British era, its roof tiled. A blackboard hung from the walls of its verandah on which names and numbers of arriving and delayed trains were written with chalk. Most of the timings of trains remained outdated, yet to be wiped out. Some of the late arrival timings had been changed several times. The constant use of the duster made the board indistinct, and the writings murky. Though I stood before the board thrice and scanned the name and number of my train, I failed to locate it. Has my train along with its number also become a part of the chalk board? But this time I had no intention of turning back. I was fast losing my patience.

Three clerks on different desks inside the office were busy filling up the gaps in the register before them. Their faces betrayed a sense of boredom usually seen amongst government employees. They simultaneously lifted their heads, as if the three heads were a part of the same body, looked towards me and then buried themselves in their work. Possibly, they were used to looking at harassed passengers like me. The station master's room was wide open, only a heavy curtain hung loosely. The station master was a middle-aged man, of wheatish complexion, with thick spectacles resting on his nose. He was sitting behind a blue painted table on which were placed a series of phone sets. His ear was on a particular receiver. The walls behind him, and on the right side, were covered with charts and maps. On the left hung a chandelier, its glass sides were half open and not cleaned for ages. Hearing the sound of my footsteps, he stops in the middle of his speech, covers the receiver with his hands, and looks at me questioningly.

'When did the platform clock stop?' I ask him. But soon I realise my blunder. What game is my unconscious self, playing with me today? 'I am sorry,' I add, 'I wanted to know about my train. I have been waiting for the last seven hours. Can you tell me when it will arrive? I am giving you its details.'

'That has left long ago,' the station master places the receiver on the cradle.

'You mean to say from the platform? But I didn't hear any announcement?' I felt the earth move below my feet.

'Didn't you see the time on the platform clock?' The station master looks at me inquiringly.

'But it has stopped.'

'Sure it did. But it's nothing new. It stopped when your train left.'

A phone rang. He picked up the receiver and talked to someone either on the up or down station, for he was using those words. I placed my suitcase on the floor and sat down on the visitor's wooden bench. Suddenly, the sense of exhaustion overtook my senses. Both my shoulders seemed numb. My body seemed like a heavy load capable of sinking through the wooden bench. What is there left for me to do? I ask myself. 'Everyone here is interested in stories. So, what is the story about?'

The station master remains on the line for a long time. Removing the receiver, a bit from his ear, he marks the chart on the wall with his pencil. He avoids some of the phone sets that ring. Sometimes he talks on a line without disconnecting the other. Sometimes he places some phones on the cradle that seem to ring with mischievous intent. He brings out registers of different sizes from the drawer, and scans them. Though his actions show his dedication to his work, I have a feeling it may be his usual trick to avoid people like me, which he must have picked up in his long professional career. Time passes making me feel as if I had never been present there at all. I was like an insect which men may cast their eyes on only to avoid.

'Hello!' My patience has reached its limits. Standing up, I bang my fist so hard on the rexine-covered table that the telephone, penholder, water bottle, glass, table calendar, and paper weight, all go for a toss. The station master places the receiver on the cradle, sits upright, catches the handles of the chair firmly and stares at me with helpless eyes.

'What does this mean, sir?' he speaks in a voice that does not seem to be his. His brows over his spectacles are stretched taut like a bow. But I do not know what storm took place in my eyes that exercised the moral pressure under which he had to lay down his weapons. His brows relax a bit. He picks up the courage to say, 'Shall I call the police?'

'Sure, call by all means,' I stare at him with wild eyes. 'With the ticket in my hand I have the right to know what happened to my train.'

'Didn't I tell you it has left?' The station master's voice became stable. 'Why don't you think of taking another train?'

'Why should I? I am not at fault. If the clock has stopped, it is your duty to see to it. What do they pay you for? Why can't you repair it? Does it not send a wrong message to the passengers especially in a country where people depend more on government institutions than even on God? And they have become accustomed to stand before government employees, their tails between legs with bated breath and sad looks?'

The station master quietly stares at me for a long time, unable to speak. Possibly, he had never faced a person like me ever. Irritated by his silence, I pick up the suitcase from the floor.

'It's useless talking to you,' I tell him. 'It's better to talk to the walls instead.'

Suddenly the station master becomes energised. He gets up from the chair and extends his hands towards me. 'You look upset,' he clears his throat. 'I can understand your problem. Had Gocharan Ray been here, he would have been of some help. He is the right man for you. He has retired today and left for his quarter with all his belongings.'

I stare at his extended hands for a while. 'Why is everyone using the name of Gocharan Ray?' I say in disagreement. 'Why should I take the help of this man?' My fingers move unconsciously on the handles of the suitcase I am carrying. 'I want to know about a train and you are directing me to your signal man? That too, when he has retired and not under you anymore?'

I hear the sounds of approaching feet near the door. Two tall uniformed men lift the curtain and stare at me. One of them has a long face, full of pimples. The second does not even have a proper face. The brass plates fixed on their caps glitter under the light of the room.

'Jadhav! No problem here,' the station master tries to ward them off. He wipes his face with a handkerchief while relaxing on the chair. He waits for a while, but when the two do not move, he loses his patience. 'I told you I can manage him. The man is upset because of the departure of his train.'

The curtain has been drawn and both of us sit quietly. Strangely, the phone sets too do not ring. The rustle of the leaves of the trees from outside sails through the open window into the stillness of the room. I fail to understand the whole episode. 'Am I a part of a deeper conspiracy which is difficult to fathom?' The silence of the room tells on my nerves. I get up and lift my suitcase. 'Strange station!' I mutter. 'There is a stopped clock here. There is a train that departs without arriving. And amongst all these mysterious things is a signal man who has retired, bears a strange name, and has been telling a strange tale to people for a long time, a tale that no one knows, is nonsensical, has neither a beginning nor an end. What is left for me except to bang my head against the walls and the pillars of the station?'

'Take my advice and postpone your trip,' the station master gets up again from his chair. He wrings both his hands as if feeling sorry for me. 'Why don't you think of taking another train? I think it is better for you to change your destination itself. When everything is going against you, it is better you tread cautiously. We are passing through a phase where we have to mark our steps, any false steps may land us in trouble.'

'Thanks,' I say, 'you are playing the role of a station master perfectly.'

I have come out with my suitcase. The shadows under the roof of the shed have disappeared. The tree by the tar-coal-coloured sun seems to have been bathed in its dying light. The platform on the other side of the railway tracks stands under the shadow of the building structure's entrance. There is a crowd of passengers and their sudden activity shows that an announcement of the arrival of a train had been made. 'Should I cross the footbridge and go to the platform on the other side? Who knows maybe the arriving train on that side could be mine?'

'What nonsense!' I become conscious of my foolishness. 'The train that arrives on that platform goes in the opposite direction. Has the earth turned on its orbit in such a manner that in order to reach my destination I have to catch the train running in the opposite direction?'

***

The sun is now behind the entrance building. I am feeling very hungry. Most probably I would be able to think properly if I eat something. I would be able to tackle the unique situation that has engulfed me from all sides; arrive at some solution to it. Lamps have been lit on the platform, but the trees standing near the tracks, and the frontispiece of the ornamentation of the station structure, still seem to be bathed in the sunlight. The inside of the canteen has been lit; its plastic-fibre tables empty, except for one, where a man, whose neck is long like the Pharaoh, is deeply engrossed with the inside of his tea cup. Winter is yet to make its appearance felt, but he has started using a printed muffler, placing it below the lower part of his neck. He is wearing torn and tattered plastic sandals out of which the toes of his feet stick out hideously. A rexine bag, bloated like a pregnant woman's stomach, is placed on his table; its handle the colour of a lighted lamp peeping out. Inside the showcase of the canteen, a plastic tray contains cake, potato *chops*, and *samosas* waiting for customers for ages. Most of the hollows of the cold-drink crate. contain empty bottles. Flies are having a field day, rubbing their bodies against the plastic straws jutting out of the empty bottles. The canteen's only waiter tries to avoid me by not making eye contact. When it becomes impossible to do so, he unwillingly comes along, his dirty towel thrown over his shoulders. He is wearing cheap, thick spectacles because of his weak eyesight, through which his eyes roll like those of an owl.

'Time for lunch is over,' he informs, 'now only cakes and *samosas* are available. Or maybe a potato *chop*.'

'Hot?'

'No. The embers of the stove have been taken off. You must have seen that after sunset there are only a few passengers in the station. It is the rules of the tender that makes us keep the shop open for some fixed hours.'

'Yes, I know,' I say, 'people in this city do not like travelling at late hours. The area is infested with robbers. Anyway, cake and hot tea will do. Tea will be hot, I suppose?'

'Why not?' the waiter smiles. 'You are right about the robbers. Last week when I was returning home at night, a man asked for a matchbox and took away my whole month's salary. He was finally caught from *cinder patti*, where till recently they deposited ashes of the steam engines. He was living in a hut with a teenage girl he brought from somewhere, and would physically abuse her at night. A week before the incident, he was having tea here, and during the conversations managed to find out when I would get my pay.'

'Nights are not meant for this city,' I sigh, 'if the sun does not set here, that would be better.'

The waiter shakes his head in agreement. He places a china plate with a chocolate-coloured cake on my table. More than a cake, it looked like a piece of dirt in the shape of a cake. He puts a china cup close to it, its mouth so small you could hardly put your finger inside it. Taking a kettle with boiled tea from the stove, he pours it into the cup and returns to the counter. He whispers something to the manager and goes out of the exit door of the canteen. Outside, water overflows from the overhead tank like a fountain, making a dog run in and out of the falling water. Probably it was enjoying every bit of it. After five minutes, when I had the cake and somehow managed to drink the overboiled distasteful tea, the waiter appears at the entrance of the canteen. With him was the same railway policeman whose face was covered with pimples and whom the station master had addressed as Jadhav.

'If you have had your tea, then can we go?' the two-starred inspector, keeping his hand on the holster of his revolver, says politely.

'Are you speaking to me?' I ask in surprise.

'Naturally. We are not speaking to the walls. We are asked to make certain enquiries about you.'

'The station master must have complained.' I take out money from my wallet, and look at the paper in which the bill amount had been scribbled with a blunt pencil.

'No. We policemen take our own decisions.'

'May I take my suitcase?'

'Why take the trouble? Noorul, pick it up,' Jadhav orders his assistant, on whose shoulder hangs a heavy rifle. His chin seems to hang too low; his hair stands on his head like a jackal.

The waiter returns with my change on a tray which I pick up and place inside my wallet. I leave a two-rupee coin on the tray as a tip. The waiter looks intently but does not pick it up. Possibly, he does not have the habit of seeing such a paltry amount on the tray. While leaving the canteen, I find the man in the muffler still seated quietly in his seat. His eyes are bereft of any feeling. Possibly we are living in an age when, for the sake of safety, it is important to present a dispassionate face.

On the deserted platform we walk between dark and semi-dark houses, resting places, an upper-class waiting room, and pass a ladies' toilet, outside of which hangs a big electric bulb. The white light shines brightly inside the waiting room, but the chairs placed in between the bright walls do not have a single passenger. We pass them and keep walking for some time on the deserted platform in the fading light of the evening. The air blows softly here and below the ghostly trees it seems like either some tramps have lit fires or the eyes of cats are glinting brightly. At last, we arrive at an old three-storeyed building which is the last one on this side of the platform, for after this the network of tracks is spread out. Apart from the spiral wooden staircase, the greater part of the building is plunged in darkness. We proceed cautiously on the steps where on a landing or two, suddenly some bulbs switch on by themselves. We reach the upper part of the building. I am taken to a room that looks like a hall; its windows hinged on casements that open on a brightly lit city. In the middle of the room stands a huge dark oval table. On it hangs a light, low and fastened with wires from the ceiling. Under the glare of the bright light, the polished surface of the table shines like a mirror though its lower parts are covered in darkness. No chairs can be seen in the hall where one can take rest. The low-watt bulbs in the brackets of the lamp shower a light on the walls that looks like the wings of butterflies.

'Is this a torture room or what?' I casually turn around to look at them. Though the surrounding was scary, I do not know why I did not feel frightened. It may be because I had become used to living in a country where the days and nights do not belong to you. As it is, what do I have to lose except a worthless life?

'Do we look like torturers to you?' Jadhav replies.

'Oh! Then I am mistaken. Actually, I have seen such a room for the first time in my life.'

'I agree,' Jadhav again replies. 'Of the many purposes of the room, it can be one of them. Even one minute ago, we have no idea of what we have to do.' He catches the table with both hands and stares into my eyes. 'So, you belong to this city?'

'Sure! I have my identity card.'

'Good. How many years have you spent in this city?'

'What do you mean? I was born and brought up here. My forefathers are buried in the burial ground of the city. You want to know how many years I have been here. Let me tell you, apart from this, I do not know any other city, though it's not close to me anymore. For me it has become an alien city.'

'Nobody contacted you on the mobile while you waited for the train, moving from one platform to the other? Or you thought of making calls to them?'

'I came out of the house without informing anyone. You can see I do not have a cell phone. I did not want my family to be able to contact me either.'

'There must be some reason. No one cuts off contact with his family like that.'

'It's a long story. The sum of the story is I have a wrong bone inserted in my body which is the cause of all ills. The city has made me a loser. I have nothing to do with it here now.'

For a moment it makes Jadhav reflective. Possibly, he was not ready for my weird story. All this while the silence of the room weighed like a heavy stone crushing the three of us under its weight. I hear the jackal-like constable whispering something.

'He is talking about some wrong bone, sir.'

Jadhav stares at him with bored eyes, visible lines appearing on his forehead. 'That's not our job,' he gives a terse reply to his assistant. He turns his head towards me and gives orders to place the suitcase on the table.

The suitcase is kept on the table. I open the combination lock. Jadhav takes out all my belongings, one by one. Looking at him I think how man may not even be conscious of when his role of professional duty changes and he returns to his inner animal nature. He takes out papers from underneath the clothes, and examines them under the bright light by squinting his eyes. It is evident that his eyesight is becoming weak but he is not conscious of it. He should visit a good ophthalmologist. After a prolonged scrutiny of my items, he probably feels dejected. He indiscriminately throws them back into the suitcase while I throughout remain withdrawn from all this, standing by the window and watching the lights of the city. I am thinking why I could not become a part of this city; its gardens, parks, ponds, markets, hotels, educational institutions. What happened that these drew themselves away from me and men tried to avoid even my shadow?

'I do not know why the city behaved in this manner with me?' I shrug my shoulders and shout at the top of my voice. I am astonished with my own voice. The fact is I was not at that time consciously addressing anyone in particular. 'I had not demanded much from the city; just my quota of oxygen.'

My reply came in the form of the sounds of footsteps on the spiral staircase. I turn my head and find myself alone in the hall. The lid of my suitcase is open. It becomes obvious that when the items were haphazardly thrown inside, the lid must have refused to shut. I rearranged everything and shut the lid noisily to make light of the weird atmosphere around me. It seemed to me that the noise had frightened some bird lying next to the window, making it fly away. But it may be my wishful thinking.

I have come out of the hall and, standing on the landing, I am trying to comprehend the spiral staircase which goes down hazily with its web-like design. The quavering shadows of the steps on the wall fall in such a way as if they cast a psychological impact on my descent.

'Hello! What is it all about?' I hold the railing of the staircase and send my voice down the hollow part of the stairway. 'Am I imprisoned here?' My voice echoes back.

Below, on a landing, a door opens and closes by itself. Far from the city, sail the sounds of firecrackers and band music; the trumpet being paramount. After all that is happening to me and under such a context, this kind of clamour seems odd. Still, I think that whatever is happening to me, and is beyond my comprehension, or whatever takes place in the life of an individual, cannot be as important as to affect the life of the whole city. On the other hand, it is not surprising that when I was undergoing the turmoil of the strange events of my life, the people of the city of my birth, through noise and violence, were trying to find some meaning of life in their respective ways. For when we fail to understand the cause of our emptiness, we fill it with din and clamour. Or to put it in a better way, when we fail to get answers to our questions, we have no options but to beat drums, shout over loudspeakers to create a din in which everything gets drowned. I was so immersed in my thoughts that I barely avoided dashing against someone on the first landing. He was holding three bottles of cold drinks in his left hand, and a paper packet in his right, from which wafted a strong smell of omelettes. He was not in uniform but must be a policeman, otherwise how can his presence be explained in such a place?

'Be careful, sir!' he smilingly says. When for no rhyme and reason someone wishes you well, he must be in the last stage of drunkenness. 'The steps of the staircase are worn out. Take small steps.'

'Thanks. I am in a hurry. I do not want to miss my train.'

Coming out of the building I find the sky full of stars, a strong wind blows, and a dog is preparing to bark at me.

***

I face the strong wind, walk in the darkness while a light seems to wait for me at some distance on the platform. I turn back to look at the building from which I have come out. The windows of the top floor are still lit as if someone is being questioned there. The dog follows me, maintaining a distance, yapping 'woof, woof' in a hushed voice. But the pace with which I am heading towards the light is similar to the distance that develops between me and the dog till it gets lost in the darkness behind me. The barking of the dog can still be heard, as if it is not the dog, but the darkness howling. My feet have become numb. A few passengers can be seen on the platform. I enter a sea of light, select a wooden seat near a painted spittoon, place the suitcase under my head, and spread my legs out. Though my eyelids feel heavy, sleep seems far away. I constantly gaze at the points of my shoes to remain awake. All kinds of thoughts come to my mind which I cannot shake off. Amongst them are also the band party and clamour of the city-dwellers, though silence reigns on the platform like at a burial ground. I keep turning on the bench for a long time. It may be the fear of someone stealing my suitcase if I fall asleep. That same fear might have made me fall into a deep sleep. In my dream, I am moving from one platform to another, looking for my stolen suitcase, when someone shakes me up violently. I wake up to find it is morning, and a train is standing close to me packed with passengers. Near all the doors of the train are crowds of passengers and others who have come to see them off. Newspaper boys and vendors pass by the windows shouting out about their wares. Close to me, from the window, someone had vomited, tracing a long line on the compartment walls.

The same coolie bends over me.

'Sir, your train has arrived and you are fast asleep. Be quick. The guard can show his green flag anytime. I have managed to bag a seat for you. Give me whatever you like.'

The coolie, without my permission, picks up my bag. I am running behind him like a robot. I can feel pain in my joints.

I have no shame in saying that I am feeling a peculiar sense of happiness in retrieving my suitcase though its loss took place in a dream. The train is long, and in between compartments, a stink spreads in the air, making it clear it must have had an overnight journey. I enter the compartment following the coolie without even enquiring whether it was my train or not. I take the seat offered to me by the coolie. I am surprised why it did not occur to me earlier that if I had no destination then I could have taken any train for that matter. When I sit back, relax, and take a deep breath, a man of short height smilingly looks at me. He is a man with no neck; to ward off the morning cold, he is wearing a grey, oversized uniform, the collars of which go up to his ears. This uniform is usually worn by railway employees in winter.

'Probably you were on the lookout for me?' he addresses me. 'You must have heard my name. I am the signal man, Gocharan Ray. Do you want to know the story about the stopped clock?'

'Is it a long story?'

'I can make it as long as you like. I can make it so long that the journey may come to an end but not the story. After all, what is the purpose of a story if it cannot help us leave time behind?'

'Then we will have a pleasant journey,' I smile and spread out my legs under the seat and look out of the window where the sun has risen from the midst of the fields and the trees are swiftly moving backwards.

AGONY

SIDDIQUE ALAM

I received a letter in which my death was forecast. The writer signed his name as Ummeed Ali. Does he know me? Yes, he has seen me many a time on the bridge near the public mausoleum, through which passes a large water pipe. I have no hesitation in saying that I like this bridge, though several beggars always sit on the pipe. Who gives them alms? I have never given any. I have never seen anyone do so. Some believe that these men, sitting on the pipe in tattered garments, are not professional beggars. Under this guise, they pursue the sale of drugs, fetch customers for the prostitutes living in *jhuggis* and huts, pickpockets of the passers-by, and are usually involved in the disappearance of unsuspecting poor children from the nearby slums. Whatever the reason, a strange sense of desolation reigns at the hind part of the bridge, where standing near the railing and watching the sunrise and the sunset is a different kind of experience. But the real fun is during the moonlit night when the stars are shining. The strange part is that in the letter there is a reference to the moonlit nights, when standing there on the bridge, I turn into a lifeless statue. But who would be interested in my life, forecasting my death, and making me aware of it by writing a letter? It was specially mentioned in the letter that my death would occur in this month itself, though Ummeed Ali had not thrown light on how I would die. Possibly he did not know it himself because if it had been known, then it probably could have been averted. After all, we are living in an age of science where, if it is not about some incurable disease, something at least can be done. Rather, now, it is possible to postpone the period of even incurable disease for a few years. No! It is fixed that death cannot be postponed; the letter reasserts with confidence. Then what made him write this letter? Is it that he wants to become famous by doing so? Was it not enough that instead of writing me the letter, he could have referred to my case and published it in some daily newspaper? Ummeed Ali! Probably I have heard this name. Is he not the same man who sells flutes at the goat market near the canal, and people take him to be a thug?

This goat market is a bit away from my lane. A reeking smell emits, though felt only at times because a large number of houses are situated between the market and our house. Standing by the side of the market, one can see thousands of goats and sheep, which the traders tie up in groups of ten. Watching these animals, the natural response of anyone would be that the city is a demon that devours thousands of animals daily with their horns and skin, and yet its hunger remains insatiable. When I went to the market with the letter looking for him, I could not find him for a few days. The floor of the market, because of the movement of animal hoofs, had been reduced to dust and dirt. Scattered dry leaves lay around that the animals had refused to partake. On the leaves, crushed by human footsteps, were also marks of animal urine, from which rose a strong stench. The bridge of the public mausoleum could be seen from the marketplace, which was the only way of crossing the canal. By the side of the canal, on the railing, hung *lungis*, beddings, and blankets, which had permanently gotten stuck to it because of sun and rain. During the morning hours, in the waters of the canal, which could better be referred to as filth, hordes of half-naked children would be seen coming out from the *jhuggis* and huts nearby, looking for fish and snails. But by afternoon, the canal would be deserted. The bigger part of the market was illegally occupied by the animal traders, who would be sitting outside their huts, built out of mats, on charpoys, having tea or talking among themselves. Finding a trader perched alone on a charpoy, I asked him about the flute player about whom he expressed ignorance. He was attired in an undergarment and kurta and held a calculator in one of his hands, on which, moving his thumb finger, he was babbling some spiritual verses. First, he expressed ignorance; then he seemed to remember.

'That thug?' he said and kept quiet. To express the rest, he spoke in a low voice. 'I think the police might have picked him up.' That was all he said.

More than a flute player, the man was notoriously known as a thug! From this it can be derived that he must have written this letter according to a plan. He might have thought that in this way, I might come under his clutches. He must have emptied the purses of many a man by instilling the fear of death. While returning home, the idea occurred to me to tear the letter and throw it away. But I did not do that. Back home, I read the letter again. It was a brief letter. The style of writing showed that the man was not much educated. I brought out the old iron trunk from under the bed. It had a wooden box that contained many old letters and documents. They were of no use now. I put the letter in the box and placed it inside the trunk. After a week, a taxi ran up the footpath of this arched bridge and crushed a person, that was me. At the time, I was standing with my hands on the iron railings of the bridge, in the dark of the night, watching the glittering stars, when I heard the sound of the screeching brakes. A flash of light was seen, something heavy dashed against my back, and I fell on the railings.

***

I lay unconscious for a month in a government hospital. Parts of the bones from my hips and spine had been fractured. A few operations were conducted. When I returned home from hospital after three months of treatment, the parts below my hips had become completely paralysed. Now my legs had become lifeless, joined to my body just like the legs of wooden dolls fixed with slender threads and tied to the rest of the body. Apparently, my legs had not changed much except that they now looked odd: some veins had dried up and sagged, others propped up, and the skin had a dull appearance. Or who knows, the legs looked like this; maybe I might not have thought it worthy to have a look at them. No one is bothered unless something happens. The slope of the rolling-pin-like thighs, the roundness of my knees, and calves whose heaviness had strangely now become light, and the other part, the softness of which had become stiff, as seen in patients; the skin under the heels, which was bearing the burden of the body, was lifeless, and now had turned soft; toes of the feet which now I fail to move, and the lump on the hind part of the leg, remained as purple as ever; all together point out to me that I had lost them forever. Thus, I had no option except to look at them and spend the rest of my life in bed. The owner of the mirror shop, in which I used to plate mirrors, customarily expressed his sympathy and with a month's salary, informed me of my dismissal, which was not surprising for me. Now I was of no use to him anymore. My wife, who from the beginning had not much expectation from me, was not surprised. She knew that I would get a wheelchair or a tricycle from some charitable trust and would be able to go to the shop of the mirror maker. I might get my old job back, or some other may be found for me. After all, I had worked there for years. Weeks elapsed, but nothing of the sort happened. A man suggested to me that I should write a letter to the MLA of my area. The MLA responded immediately by expressing his sympathies and enkindled my hope by an assurance that they would do something for me as early as possible. He did not take much time to fulfil his promise. Within two months, in a programme with other disabled people, I was handed a tricycle whose paddles with their cranks were fixed to the top and which I could move with my hands.

When I first sat on the tricycle, I felt that I had become a man who, in place of his feet, had developed paddles. At the back of the tricycle was engraved the name of the trust, whose proprietor was the MLA. I did not take much time to use the tricycle, for I knew how to ride a bicycle. It was only in the beginning, while ascending or descending that I had to take the help of someone. My wife was performing this duty perfectly well. In the meantime, my wife, who had studied up to class eight in an Urdu medium school, started working in a Xerox shop. My two children went to a corporation school, where they were provided with lunch.

'I am sure I would be able to be of some help,' I told my wife, 'you cannot shoulder so much burden alone.'

'Do not venture far away from home,' my wife replied without understanding my feelings. 'As it is, there are enough problems at home.'

'But both my hands are still safe,' I made a weak protest.

My wife remained quiet for a while and then replied: 'See what you can do?'

I rang up the mirror maker and requested him for a job. He asked me to come sometime in the coming week. He is a nice person and will certainly find some work for me. After calling him, a sense of peace came over me. There was still enough time before the sun would set when my wife returned from work. This was not the time for her return. She looked very tired. I asked for help from my wife to get on to the tricycle. She handed me the cooking stove in a cloth bag. It was not working properly, and a smell of kerosene was emanating from the cooked food.

'Don't be worried,' I said. 'I will bring it repaired when I return.'

The repair man asked me for an hour's time. The boy who worked for him had gone somewhere. He knew me. His eyes were full of pity for me. His wooden shop, a distance away from the entrance to the bridge, was close to the walls of the hind part of the public mausoleum. He would repair all kitchen utensils that were capable of being repaired. I had an hour at hand, for I could not return without the stove. Without it, we would have to fetch dinner from some eatery.

'I'll return from a stroll on the bridge,' I said to the shopkeeper holding the tricycle handlebars placed in front for the convenience of the occupant. I turned the tricycle towards the bridge. It was a steep climb. To reach the middle, I had to exert myself. I was panting. Once, bending for a long time over the crank of the paddle, it seemed I would lose the grip, or its chain would come out of its rounded holds, in which case it was possible that the tricycle could slide back, descend fast, and I become a victim of another accident. But I did not lose heart. I somehow managed to bring up the tricycle to the middle, where the ground was uniform. I stopped the cycle and, steadying my breathing, surveyed the railings on both sides. I understood that now the bridge was of no use to me. On one side, the pipe encompassed the largest part of the walkway, and the footpath on the other side was half a foot high. It was impossible to trundle up the tricycle on it. All kinds of vehicles were plying on the street. Nobody was allowed to halt on the way. Naturally, spotting me, a policeman came blowing his whistle. Probably he felt that by stopping there, I might start begging for alms.

Ah! I thought. Now this bridge is of no use for me except for crossing the canal. Making a U-turn, I changed the direction of the tricycle towards my *mohalla*. At that time, a gust of wind blew in which was the mixed smell of the goat market and the canal. I do not know why, maybe because I had enough time or going down the slope, my tricycle had gathered speed; its handle moved left on its own, as it sometimes happens, and within minutes I was on the road to the goat market.

That day, there was a tremendous rush at the goat market. I was thinking of returning when the sound of the flute reached my ears.

***

The advantage of a disabled person's tricycle is like that of an ambulance. People give it the right of way. Naturally, despite the crowd, it did not take me time to reach the flute player. He was a 14-year-old boy with knitted brows. He wore an old cane hat that was bigger than the size of his head. Standing under a wooden pole with a bagful of flutes on his shoulders, he was playing the flute. Finding me staring enkindled his hopes of me being a prospective customer. He took out a black flute and extended it to me.

'Are you Ummeed Ali?' I said, holding the flute.

'I am his son, sir.'

'Your father doesn't come here?'

The boy stopped on the way to placing the flute to his lips.

'You know him?'

'I want to meet him.'

'Then you have to come home with me.'

'Where do you people stay?'

'Close by, at a *mohalla*.'

I looked up to the sky, which had turned grey.

'Today, I do not have the time. As it is, after dark, I do not venture out.'

'It's alright,' the boy said, shaking his head. 'I come here every day before the sun sets.'

The boy put the flute to his lips. He was not playing any special tune. It was obvious he did not know how to play the flute. He was just trying to put the sound of the flute into some kind of a tune.

Darkness had spread all over when I reached home with the stove. I dragged out the trunk from below the bed with the help of my wife and brought the letter that had made the prediction. I read the letter many a time under the glare of the light. Though the prediction had proved to be wrong, but on the whole, it could not be said to be erroneous. I had come out of the jaws of death. Seen dispassionately, my present state of life was worse than death.

'You didn't talk of any letter before?' my wife said taking the letter.

Her eyes widened as she went on reading. 'You have never told me about this letter before,' she repeated her words.

'What difference would that have made?'

'We could have taken advice from someone. It is clear that the accident is a kind of a warning.'

'Months have elapsed since the accident,' I said taking back the letter. 'What more is left in it.'

'No. It has not passed. You have to be cautious.'

I put the letter inside the wooden box and closed the lid of the trunk. 'Now I am not scared of death.'

'How can you say this?' My wife was staring with disapproving eyes. 'You have two children. You have no compassion for them?'

I was taken aback. Her tone and tenor had changed while staying in the company of men folk. This was the woman who, till recently, could not think beyond her kitchen. Probably the saying is true: 'During bad times, a man's good qualities become prominent.'

The next day the mirror maker rang me on my mobile. He asked me to meet him. The distance I used to cover in minutes by bus took me more than half an hour. Firstly, I did not have the experience of crossing a main road on a tricycle. Secondly, moving the paddle with one hand and controlling the handlebar with the other was different from an ordinary cycle and an unusual kind of experience. Probably, that was why I felt scared when crossing the bridge to arrive at the main road. I had to negotiate between the large wheels of the buses and lorries. I was forced to move the tricycle at a snail's pace.

A sergeant controlling the traffic became impatient with my slow speed. He came blowing his whistle and stood before me.

'With this, you should not have come out at this hour,' he said, stopping traffic on both sides. 'You should have known schools close at this hour.'

'It was a compulsion, sir,' I expressed my gratitude.

From the street, I entered the lane of the mirror maker. The mirror maker met me with warmth. Other staff members also came to meet me.

The mirror maker said: 'The entire plating of the mirror is done on the ground. It's impossible to constantly change positions during work.'

'If I am provided a table, I can do the work,' I offered the suggestion. 'My wheels can move in all directions.'

But the mirror maker's view was different. He thought that I could not work without taking the help of someone. During work, large pieces of mirrors had to be taken from one place to another, which was not possible for me to handle. There was also the possibility of mirrors breaking up.

'My workshop is small,' he said. 'We work in the traditional way. Even the smallest of losses can have devastating effects on business. But don't worry. I had a talk with a *bidi* firm.'

I shook my head. 'I do not know how to bind *bidi*s.'

'It's easy,' the mirror maker said. 'You'll pick it up quickly. You'll get *bidi* leaves, tobacco and thread. You are lucky to have a tricycle. You can take your work home. The more you work, the more money you get.'

'I will work hard,' I said with determination.

'I know you will,' the mirror maker said, moving his hands over me with affection. 'You have not lost heart even after such an accident. People like you are an example for society.'

That day when I returned, with me was a bag on the seat tied to the cycle's frame. For a start, I was given little material. I was given training on how to cut leaves with scissors, and fold and fill them with tobacco. There was a special way of closing the tip and tying it with a thread. They knew that I would learn the work at home. My wife was glad to see the material. She said: 'This will make you stay at home. A way of earning has also been found.'

'It's the result of the kindness of my former boss,' I said.

'Be cautious on the main road. Accidents always take place nowadays.'

'I will learn to ride at a slow speed soon,' I smiled to wave away her fear. 'I am not the only one on a tricycle on those streets.'

The new job, in a sense, succeeded in moving my attention away from the letter and its writer. Soon I had achieved enough expertise in the art of folding *bidi* leaves. Maybe nature had supplemented fully for the non-functioning of my legs by making my fingers extra functional.

'You have proved yourself to be a good worker,' the workshop manager said, handing me the weekly income.

'That is because I am left with these two hands to which I must devote my focus and energy.'

'It's all from Allah,' he said. He was a man who was committed to fasting and prayers and had full faith in God. 'Whatever God takes away with one hand; he doubly returns with the other.'

Though not truly applicable in my case, I was thankful to God. It could have been even worse. I kept praying to God for the safety of my hands. Now I had forgotten to worry about the letter. The animal market was merely a stinking place I had to face while passing through. But now I was the last man to go there.

Six months had passed since the theft took place at our house. The children had been to school. I had gone out when somebody stole the trunk from under the bed and took it away. Though the trunk contained nothing valuable, I do not know why the loss of the letter scared me.

'You are unnecessarily becoming worried,' my wife tried to calm me down. 'Your fear is justified. Now our worst days are over. That was a mishap going to happen.'

'I do not know,' my voice was weak, 'I should have burnt that letter. I should not have put a lock on the trunk. The thief might have thought it contained valuable items.'

I tried to forget the episode by getting involved in work. But slowly, a strange transformation took place in me. Not only did the speed of my work slow down, but my fingers also trembled. It seemed that something bad was going to happen, or some supernatural element would overpower me. There had also been a sudden upsurge of traffic on the street. It was becoming difficult to steer the tricycle clearly. Maybe for the petrified one in me, all these things were slowly becoming terrifying. I saw a remarkable change in treatment of the policemen as if I was unnecessarily creating hurdles in their work.

'How did the voltage become so low?' I thought one day while looking at the bulb hanging from the line. Our one-room rented house had only one small window. It was five feet above the ground. On the other side, at a handshaking distance, was the neighbour's four-storeyed illegal building. It had no source of airing or windows. So, our house had little natural light. We had to switch on the electric bulb even during the day.

'You have to talk to the electrician,' I told my wife, returning from work.

The electrician was in connivance with the employees of the electricity department. He would supply illegal connections to the people of the *mohalla*.

'I'll clean it,' my wife brought out the bulb and scrubbed it with a piece of cloth. Then she poured drops of water on it to make it shine. The bulb sparkled, but the filament got damaged. We had to buy a new bulb from the market. It made the light brighter. But it was still not to my satisfaction.

'I think you should consult an eye specialist,' my wife advised me.

'Now what's happened to my eye?' I became angry. 'I am hardly 30 years old. Why don't you talk to the electrician?'

'I did. He said the voltage is alright. We are unnecessarily complaining.'

'He's a scoundrel, power thief,' I replied but then kept quiet, for if he stopped supplying power, we would have to use the lantern. He treated these matters seriously. There are scores of people in our *mohalla* who, though living in a city glittering with lights, have to make use of the lanterns.

'See yourself. Your work is not like before,' the manager said one day placing the bundles of *bidi*s on the table. 'They say your fingers tremble. This is not the age.'

'Maybe I have to see an eye specialist,' I said, my head bowed.

'You said you have no problem with your eye.'

'I know, still, it is good to see an eye specialist.'

The eye specialist examined my eye through a computerised machine. Then asked me to read the letters placed on the wall before declaring that my eyes had no problem.

'Still, I am prescribing some medicines,' he said, 'three drops every morning and evening.'

While returning home, I remained quiet. The evening had descended, but I did not switch on the light. When my wife returned and switched on the light, she looked at me with astonishment.

'Why are you sitting in the dark? Where are the children?'

'I didn't like this sudden light,' I replied. 'The children might be playing outside.'

'What's the matter with you,' my wife said, sitting by my side. She was trying to bring out something from her bag.

'Something has gone wrong with my tricycle. It has slowed down. I have to exert a lot.'

Probably my wife had succeeded in finding the thing she was looking for. Still, her hand was inside the bag.

'Why don't you show it to a cycle mechanic,' she said.

'I did. He did the necessary work. But it is still like that.'

'Are you okay?' my wife brought out her hands from the bag and sympathetically placed them on my shoulders.

'I do not know,' my eyes were full of tears. 'Something is wrong somewhere.'

Yes. Something has gone wrong that I am unable to comprehend. What is happening to me? With the trembling of fingers, now the pressure of the rings of the scissors has added painful bruises to the joints of my fingers. They give such burning sensations that I have to take out the scissors with the other hand and am forced to throw them away. I am unable to work for long. During work, objects before my eyes turn into hazy lines, and I start mixing them up. The winter has yet to make its appearance, but I have started feeling a cold sensation. Most of the time, in the loneliness of night, I sit shivering on the bed. I do not wake up my wife fearing that I will have to give explanations. Passing by the bridge on the way to the *bidi* factory, sometimes the sound of the bell of the tricycle seems to get lost. I twist the bell hard and become tired. As a result, I stare vacantly for hours at things before me as if I lack the capacity for understanding.

'And how did the smell of the goat market start coming from the window? Before, it was never in our gully.' Slowly, without wishing it, I had started living amidst an environment of sick people.

The day I almost came under the trailer, laden with an empty canister, its uncountable wheels jumping on the street's craters, I decided to give up the job. I could not accomplish much and the factory manager was beginning to dislike my work.

'Do you think I have opened a charitable trust?' he roared in anger one day. 'You are spoiling the items. And then ask for remuneration? Why are you not working properly?'

'I am trying.'

'Yes, you try to spoil the things.'

My wife did not like my leaving the job.

'You are becoming lazy,' she said angrily. 'Have become used to an easy life. These trembling of fingers and short-sightedness are drama.'

'I will find some other job,' I said in my defence.

'There can hardly be any other job for you in the world.'

Maybe she was right. Now my heart had started beating faster. From time to time, strange sounds ring in my ears as if many people were shouting far away from a microphone. Now I fail to sit on the tricycle by myself, though I had developed expertise in it. With little exertion, I start panting. For the last few weeks, I have seen ants crawling on my skin, which made me develop the habit of continuously dusting my clothes. Both my children think it to be funny but do not express themselves because of my hot temperament. I do not know why I cannot sleep. Spread out on the bed, night after night, I stare at the window placed high up through which nothing can be seen except for the neighbour's wall. But staring for long, the window acquires the form of a letter from which words drop down like withered leaves. I try to read the words but shadows form in my eyes, and the words vanish.

***

For the last two weeks, I have been going around the goat market. But the boy with the flute could not be seen.

'For the last few days, I have seen you come here on your tricycle,' a trader said one day.

He was smoking a hookah, perched on the charpoy near the railings. 'What do you want? You don't come to buy animals?'

'I am on the lookout for a boy who sells flutes.'

'Have tea,' he said, looking towards the tea vendor, who was pouring tea from the kettle into a plastic cup.

'No, I just need the address of that boy. Do you know his name?'

'Mukarram Ali. That was what he told me. I do not know him. Do you know him?' the trader asked the tea vendor.

'I do not know where he lives,' the tea vendor replied. 'He lives close by. I have seen him sell flute near the large *nullah*.'

The information was of no use to me. I stopped going to the market and, on my tricycle, started making rounds of the *mohalla*s near the canal. Most of the lanes here were narrow, where people would stand as if they had no work at hand. It was just like my *mohalla*, and because I was in no hurry, I did not find it difficult to navigate my cycle. My wife knew nothing about this quest. She was under the impression that I was wandering in search of a job. She would go out early in the morning for her job and return before sunset. Nowadays, she had become irritable, for the financial burden temporarily eased by my job had returned to her. I had stopped having lunch. This was the way of helping my wife financially. To disregard the demands of hunger was not easy. Slowly I became used to it. Nowadays, I do not feel hungry during the daytime. Now I had also come to know why men who sit in tricycles take to begging. Not only do they get alms, but the giver also feels satisfied they have given it to the right person. I have strictly tried to avoid asking for alms, though now very little money was left with me. Maybe because my only expenditure now was restricted to having tea and *bidi*s. The habit of smoking *bidi*s was the result of my previous job.

I should ring up the mirror maker. He may be able to find some other job for me. But how can I do any work when every part of my body is conspiring against me? Even during daytime nowadays, darkness descends before my eyes as if the sun is a bulb whose voltage is becoming dimmer day by day. The flute player can only help me out of it. He had started the whole affair by writing the letter to me. I started looking for him. I ransacked all the *mohalla*s near the canal. I knew the large *nullah* that the tea vendor had talked about. I do not know where this dirty *nullah* goes slithering like a snake between sheds. It looked as if all *mohalla*s of the town were situated along its bank. The lifestyle of the people living here is the same. It is only while passing through the main road that life looks different. Otherwise, there are tiled roofs, narrow lanes, crowds of people, unnecessary noise from loudspeakers, and chaos. At last, one day, amid the bedlam, I succeeded in finding him out. Or maybe, it is better to say that he succeeded in finding me out.

The sun, like the spider's net, had become hazy. Or maybe, my eyes were to be blamed. It must have rained in some parts of the city, making the air cool. Sitting on the tricycle, I managed to wear a sweater with shaking fingers. Nowadays, I use to keep this sweater with me. There were certain big holes in the sweater, which I tried to mend through woollen threads sloppily. I was moving by the edge of the *nullah*, thronged by people who had nothing to do, when in the dirty waters, I spotted the carcass of an animal, over which was a horde of crows. While I mused about the carcass that had been dumped, the sound of the flute was heard, and my ears pricked up.

This voice was coming from some nearby hut. I went around looking on my tricycle. But before I could locate it, the sound stopped. A dwarf, whose age was difficult to ascertain, was sitting on the threshold of a closed shop, staring at me for some time. He beckoned me towards him.

'You are looking for Ummeed Ali?'

'Yes! I am looking for his house.'

'Can you see the lane there, at the mouth of which stands the trolley of the sugarcane *wallah*? The house of Ummeed Ali is inside the lane. From the entrance, on the right side, after three houses, you will find a tin door.'

The lane was extremely narrow, entering which made it difficult to turn the tricycle around. I entered nonetheless without thinking of the consequences. Reaching the door, I raised my hands to knock when the door opened. The boy with the knitted brows was standing before me.

'Do you remember me? 'I said.

'Come in,' the boy stepped aside from the door.

He brought out a plastic stool and placed it on the threshold. I got up from the tricycle and, with the boy's help, sat on the stool. For the sake of balance, I held on to the threshold. Compared to the light outside, the inner part of the house appeared to be dark. Then slowly, the murky appearance cleared, and I was capable of seeing things. Close to the wall, on a wooden bed, sat a man staring at me. It was because of his bushy beard and hair that only the upper part of the visage was visible, through which his eyes shone brightly. Both his hands seemed severed from his shoulders. His legs were spread out; the pyjamas tucked up to his knees. A woman kept massaging his legs with oil. At the corner sat a young girl on the floor on a piece of rexine, stringing plastic *moti*s under the light of a zero-watt bulb. On the walls, at several spots hung clothes from nails emitting a foul smell. It looked like they were not clothes but human skeletons listening to our conversations, dangling from the walls. Bags, from which flutes of different sizes stuck out like sticks, hung from the roof. The bright light filtering through a missing tile from the roof spread like blistering fluid.

'My son told me about you, but it relates to an old incident,' the man without shoulders signalled the woman to stop massaging by shaking his head. The woman pulled his pyjamas from his knees down to his ankles. She picked up the utensil of oil and went into the kitchen. The hair thrown down his shoulders, and the fishtail-like beard, made the man sitting on the wooden bed look like a masterpiece of nature, a magnum opus, to which nature had forgotten to provide shoulders. He was staring at me with wet eyes.

'What do you want from me?'

'You are Ummeed Ali?'

'Yes.'

'So, you made the forecast by writing the letter that I am going to die within a month?'

'Both my hands are cut off,' he replied. 'How can I write any letter? Can I see that letter?'

'There was a theft at my house. The thief had taken away the trunk where I had kept the letter. Didn't you write that letter?'

Instead of replying, he kept staring at the walls.

'How long is this event that you are talking about?' he asked after a short interval without looking at me.

'Ten months must have passed by.'

'But you are still living.'

'Within a week after getting the letter, I met with an accident. The lower portion down my waist has become paralysed.'

'But the letter talked about your death. You are alive.'

'Forget about that. Tell me whether you wrote that letter or not?'

'See, you must be under some mistaken notion,' he looked at me. 'Thank God that you are still alive.' He pointed to his severed shoulders by signalling with his head. 'Look at me. I am not even capable of cleaning myself.'

'Did you also meet with an accident?'

'I lied to a man. He awarded me this punishment.'

'Such a punishment? For a lie? That must have been a big one.' I could not hide my sense of humour.

'Believe me! In the business of drugs, it is normal. I have committed a number of sins in my life. Something like this was bound to happen.'

I surveyed his room. 'You are not a bad man. If you were, then you should have had wealth.'

The man bowed his head so low that the upper part of his shoulders looked like a bundle of bushy hairs.

'I was bad, even for my family members,' his eyes were full of tears.

'Abbu!' his son interrupted, and he became quiet.

'What was the reason behind the writing of that letter?' I asked for the last time.

'Why can't you understand? Abbu's hands had been cut off a year ago,' the boy said, lifting his voice.

The boy was angry with me. I sat quietly. Maybe he was also telling a lie. Maybe he was trying to help his father. But what could I do? I had no proof. Both his hands were cut off, and I had lost the letter.

When I came out, in the lane, near the *nullah*, among the idle mongers stood a seller of balloons, their colours more colourful. The dwarf, sitting on the shop edge, was missing. Turning the paddle of the tricycle under a sky where the sun was dead for me, I thought I was not the only one in the world who was unfortunate. What the letter forecasted had proved to be true. There are many other kinds of death beyond the meaning that we usually know: death, which a large number of people living under the sky are experiencing.

THE WEDDING REGISTER

SIDDIQUE ALAM

You will find piles of old books and writing copies in my house. One or two odd things, too, like the wedding register of Pinki Salman. I bought it from a scrap dealer's shop. Who is Pinki Salman? If you believe the contents of the register, he may, more or less, be the imam of a masjid or a *qazi*, or someone below him, amongst the many *moulvi*s, who besides charging the legal fees of conducting a *nikah*, will not hesitate to demand a large sum of money. The register shows that in the many *nikah*s he had conducted, in place of the signatures of agents and witnesses, were his signatures. The first signature was on 16 February 1956, and the last was on 3 June 1973. In these 17 years, Pinki Salman had conducted 1,353 *nikah*s.

Is he still living? Or has he made his eternal abode under some unmarked grave! I do not know why the register casts an influence over me, making me helplessly go in the quest of Pinki Salman.

***

It does not mean that I will go in search of Pinki Salman. By saying so, have I thrown cold water on your hopes? Or it does not matter to you whether I go in search of him or change my mind about the man. If I say that Pinki Salman was Chinese by race, one who remained happy and wanted others to be so, he who ran away from a Chinese ship at the Khidderpore dock to seek refuge in a Muslim *mohalla*, became a Muslim at the hands of a *moulvi*, and spent his whole life in the propagation of his new religion, then you may question that for a Chinese person, language must have been a hurdle. But a question can arise in your mind about his age when he converted to Islam. Had his circumcision ceremony been performed? Did he follow any religion before conversion? Or had he given up everything in that independent ship during the stormy days? If a question can be raised about his Chinese race, similarly, you can put questions on other aspects relating to him. For till the writing of this piece, apart from hearsay as proof of whatever had been stated above, there is nothing that can shed light about Pinki Salman. Or, prove his existence. Or, turn him into fiction. So, the problem is whether Pinki Salman existed or he didn't. I do not possess solid proof of those days, especially in a city where people change houses as pawns on a chess board, or where there is no ordered system of passing information, where the presence of people may not count more than their names. To say that you have said the last word in favour or against Pinki Salman is like grasping the essence of time and history and having truth in the palm of your hands.

***

Where the stony pathways were difficult to negotiate between old mansions and trees drilled with pegs on which hung tarpaulins of beggars and hawkers, there stood an old historic masjid from where I came out, holding my slippers in hand. Its patio was the precursor of mansions where once stood phaetons and hackney carriages. But those days were gone. Once where stood Ford, Humber, Buick, Baby Austin, Studebaker and other foreign-made vehicles, now rested their remains, the wheels stuck inside the mud. Bats and silence had made their abode in the mansions; most of the parts had been overtaken by land sharks and men, who perched on comfortable cushions. That day was not a significant one for me. I do not know why I thought that if I had to spend the rest of my days meaningfully, I must turn away from the beaten track, treading on which had forced me to compromise with the ups and downs of life. And, what was the way? It was just a way to exist, oblivious of whether I managed to have a piece of the sky over my head or ground beneath my feet. Those were the days when I had become used to visiting a particular scrap shop that sold old books and other scrap items. Now for me, new books had outlived their worth; their heavy vocabulary was difficult for me to hold on to, whereas the scraps of paper were bestowed with a new meaning, just like old ideas rejected with time, stick somewhere, and come into view with a new significance.

I returned home and closed the door, made the register stand on the lattice of the window so that its pages remained opened on both sides. The register was thick and oversized in length, and if one had to carry it, it could span from the neck to the hip. It had covered the full width of the window. Its unique leather cover must have given it the look of the hind part of an animal from the other side of the window. The height of the window was double the size of the register. From the upper part of the lattice was visible the ashen blue sky of a city where kites and crows flew as if sculptors had moulded them with a chisel and a hammer, but looked lacklustre because of the distance. For me, this cast a spell, and for a while, I forgot the register. Then the number of kites and crows decreased and the sky presented a layer that was a bizarre, grey whitish colour; a white that is seen when life oozes out of a body. Now, when nothing remained in the sky, I avoided it. My eyes stopped on to the slithering pages of the register where shimmering words and text seemed to appear as if dipped in water, the ink dissolving. This stain turned into mist seen on the seas in bad weather where the dim light of steamers itself becomes a part of the murky waters. It seemed as if a city existed on the surface of the water, just like cities on earth. I was trying to gauge the mist when slowly it started to move and did not take time to twist and turn where lines, words and oblong text encircled before vanishing. I was watching this bizarre maelstrom with astonishment when I spotted a staircase piercing fast through the whirlpool, like the ladders of a fire brigade heading upwards.

I had hardly come out of this spell when the wedding register disappeared from my sight. I was standing on the lower part of the stairs.

THE FIRST STAIRCASE

This staircase contained 20 steps. Though they were bound from wall-to-wall, the moment one stepped, the feeling of coarseness and unevenness were imparted to the soles of the feet. The good thing was my meeting with Pinki Salman took place at the end of the first staircase. He was waiting for me. I noticed that surprisingly he had no beard, which was not strange for a Chinese. But the astonishing part was that his face did not look like that of an ordinary human being. But it is not possible to arrive at a concrete conclusion about his face. Without knowing the history of a man, how can one say that he was Chinese or African, Turkish or Dutch? Again, to arrive at a conclusion, some light has to be thrown but that, instead of bringing out the truth about things, tends to change their identities. In our day-to-day life, what can be derived from someone's face is how long he has stayed in a geographical region. That transforms faces in a particular manner. So, we have to react to these accordingly.

So, Pinki Salman was standing at the end of the staircase. He was a Chinese whom the damp weather must have tried its best to change. Much of his self had remained inside his skin. I had to make use of these before weather and the soil of the earth may render him useless for me. When we descended from the semi-dark verandah to the open, there stood an ancient pillar. The dome above the niche had fallen apart, through which the blue parts of the sky were visible. Dry leaves moved on our path, and shadows of unseen trees slithered on walls and open spaces. It did not take me much time to understand that even below, as above, there was an abandoned world. We were walking amidst ancient and dilapidated buildings, ones that we had left above. And as above, walking in between the ruins of the buildings was proof of their existence. After walking for a distance, we arrived at a blue water tank; its walls busted in places. I noticed that the water was normal, but the tiles at the bottom made it look azure. Pinki Salman sat down on the walls of the tank. He put his hands into the water, played with it and enquired about me. Though he spoke in Urdu, every word proved his Chinese ethnicity. I told him on the first staircase that I had lost my past, without which the identity of an individual becomes meaningless. For whatever we want to know about a man, we know it from his past, that which is dead and gone. Naturally, for the resumption of my past, it was necessary that I should go to look for it.

Pinki Salman tried to laugh. He said that the obsolete marriage register must have come into my hands. For a moment, his weak teeth became visible. It made me think about the Chinese dentists who are now becoming extinct. He informed me that the object of the staircase I had selected to reach him was nothing except to make my way lengthier. I stared at him with astonishment. Was the labyrinth of buildings where we squatted just a maze, its object to transform his identity into fiction? Can it be that the last key of this magical world was not even in the hands of Pinki Salman, he himself standing in between me and the truth like a maze? Then why was it that he did not come to show me the way? He pointed to the sky, a part of which was still bright like a wound that had burst itself, its pus oozing out. With reflected thoughts, he nodded, exposing his weak teeth. It did not take me much time to understand that his smile meant nothing. On the other hand, whatever there was in between the earth and the sky, its beginning and end were proving to be wrong. Then he searched his pockets and brought out some Chinese coins. He told me that they had come in handy during bad days. They helped him come out alive when his ship came into the jaws of the sea dragon and he lost everything.

Now what was the need to become a Muslim? He put it in such a way as if he wanted me to accept that the question should have been asked by me. But when he saw no interest in me, he became quiet.

I was getting involved in some important work. I was trying to assess the ruins all around me. I was beginning to understand that whatever was seen, including the coins in the hands of Pinki Salman, its worth was of numismatic value only and was nothing but a mirage. I understood that the man was not passing down information; he was placing hurdles between them. Probably he had read my thoughts. He understood that I possessed a head over my shoulders which I was forced to carry with me. He put the coins inside his pockets. He brought out a cap, put it on and said that the sun may go down at any time. God was in his heaven, watching everything—God, who had either created man too late or before time, rendering him unfit for any work. I was watching him in astonishment. He stood up and, without shaking hands with me, entered the tank. He waded in knee-deep waters and vanished in the dark. A question may arise as to why I did not pursue the man. It may be because I knew that this was not the right time, for he had to cross many a distance between man, the universe and God. This pursuit of mine would have been something much before time.

When I arrived at the staircase in order to return, I was stunned. Several naked men were descending the steps and vanishing inside demolished buildings. I was not surprised at their nakedness, for this was the picture that the pages of the register tried to show rather than the holy verses with which their nudity was being hidden. My inner voice told me that their movement may not come to an end. They were men who were related to Pinki Salman's marriage register and now their generations had started multiplying. Undoubtedly the man must have been watching the game, standing somewhere, until I lay down my weapon. My voice also told me that possibly this was not the time for my return. It was not because I did not want to return. But this staircase, where the continuous descent of men would never come to an end, was not meant for return. Should I go back to the demolished houses to see whether these people who were descending had faith in those structures? Or whether they were leading lives according to the oath they had taken? It was also to prove whether my mind was capable of anything.

THE SECOND STAIRCASE

Behind the discovery of this second staircase, through which I wanted to make my entry into the buildings where those men were entering, lies a story. A friend of mine, who was of Fidel Castro's age, challenged and said that what we think as above and below was, in fact, an assumption. If we keep in mind all the sides of the universe, then the idea of up and down becomes meaningless. People thought that my friend was not capable of finding anything new except what lay immediately before him. Presuming that men may not take him seriously, my friend of Castro's age burnt all the papers on which he had worked for so many years. As a result, his house was burnt and turned to ashes. He lost his memories and both his eyes. But the fire made men conclude that if one loses his memory and eyes, then there will be nothing left to prove right or wrong. That the world is as the eyes see it; memory gives shape to it. Thus, my friend of Castro's age had unravelled a puzzle that increased his worth in the eyes of the public. So, while searching for the second staircase, I remembered my friend. Both my eyes became capable of seeing better. I spotted strange stairs that went up and down simultaneously. There was a challenge waiting on each step, making one feel either one inch above or one inch below sea level. That is, whatever distance one was covering, one was losing it with the same speed. Standing on one such step, I saw the sky above where the steps had ended. The sky could also be seen below, where the stairs ended. As if both the points had conspired, even the shining stars seemed to have become a part of this conspiracy. It seemed that reality lay in between the steps of the two staircases. I tried to remember Pinki Salman. Someone has to unravel the mystery of my friend; otherwise, I may never be able to reach Pinki Salman.

I spotted Pinki Salman, who was simultaneously ascending and descending at the same time. When he came close to hand-shaking distance, I turned around to see him behind me. He was present both above and below me. It was difficult to give him a single face. To understand whether he was two or one individual, I tried to change my position. But every time, I spotted the same Pinki Salman. Has radiance on the earth changed altogether?

Direction was not necessary for travel. Pinki Salman was so close that he could smile and shake hands with me. We sat down there, for walking and sitting had lost meaning for us. When I looked at him, he looked younger than before. Was this second meeting an incident that took place before the first? Or was it that here too, the matter was something different? Why was he erecting hurdles in the way of reaching out to him? The world was not his creation, but he had lived a long life. He must have some knowledge, like my friend, who, after losing his eyesight and memory, had reached a part of the truth, which, whether you accept it or not, was worth discussing.

The floor on which we sat was made of fire bricks and thus looked entirely black. A large number of rats ran all around. But in their scurry, there was a sense of commonness, a weird kind of boredom, as if their movements had been restricted.

Pinki Salman said that it was wrong, for no cat had been created for them.

How is that possible? Why is it that Pinki Salman is in the know of things that are of no use to me? I saw him sitting with his fingers crossed on his big tummy. That means he was a denizen of the world that had invented the toilet. But I do not know why the idea occurred to me that all my attempts at making Pinki Salman open his mouth would go in vain, for whatever he was going to utter related to my mind, to the extent that it would just enhance the areas of doubt.

Pinki Salman's eyes were hard like glass but hazy. Staring into my eyes he said: 'Maybe you might be thinking whether a man who wished good for others had ever seen a woman.'

This thought had not come to me. Suddenly, I remembered that the thought had been with me the day I had discovered the register. My superiority complex made me commit the mistake of looking at the register from the point of view of the dead men, where women are seen only to the extent we want to see them. Ah! Pinki Salman, man of few words; his silence carries bundles of curses. On the other hand, we crazy guys are interested in words, forgetting that they create only noise.

Pinki Salman pointed to the ups and downs of the staircases (apologies for the terminology), where long queues of women moved up and down but were devoid of faces, eyes, noses, or mouths. It was strange that every woman was simultaneously seen moving up and down. In case of a collision, they merged into one another and disappeared from view.

Pinki Salman was watching me closely. He said that all women lost their identities on the day he entered their names in the register. Later on, he came to know that the date of entry was the last day of their lives. The women got lost, as if their existence had been wiped out.

Pinki Salman got up and started to move up the stairs. Without a thought, I stared down below. He, without a beard, had lost his identity like the women. His disappearance amongst women was proof that since men emerge out of women, they know no other way out. All our lives, we search for the same way of entrance. What else does the presence of the register tend to prove?

THE THIRD STAIRCASE

To know the truth about a thing is only possible when we stand up without any support. For the other object becomes a part of our selves and changes our point of view. As a result, we lose the truth about the object. I became conscious of it while standing amidst the uncountable staircases which, either was one, which different points of view had transformed into thousands or had been thousands, which from a single point and my vision of singularity, appeared to be one. But now, since I have come so far, or so close, will I be able to find Pinki

Salman amongst the staircases? It is also possible that by now, he might have changed his face altogether. Whatever might have been left, he might have been capable of hiding them. After all, how long can you remain aloof from the influences of people, air, and earth?

Pinki Salman found the solution to the problem by searching me out. Now, I could hear his voice. I could not see him. Was he playing a game with me from the outset?

It is not that like God I am present everywhere, and impossible to have me in your grip, he was saying. To grasp me, you do not even have to open your palms. On board the ship, I saw it in the eyes of the dragon. It was possible, for I saw to that extent. You can describe my whole story in a few words.

I was getting angry with the man. What was the need for this? When was I trying to steal him from himself? Was I destroying him, bit by bit, and to save himself he had taken this route? As far as God is concerned, I never treated him as a problem. I do not know whether I myself had been created. Or, someone else is thinking me out.

I tried to put my feet on the first step, thinking that without that, it was not possible to reach the man. Instead of something concrete, my feet dangled in the air. I got saved somehow. Now it dawned that what I had seen were not staircases at all. I heard Pinki Salman's laughter. It was meant to throw cold water on my hopes. I was becoming angry with him for no reason. He may not be the designer of the spell. What is the worth of a *qazi* that I should think he was the source of it all. Then I thought that if the laughter was of Pinki Salman, he must be around. I wanted to stay away from the innumerable staircases but both their sources were submerged in a haze. It was bizarre. Wherever I went, I found myself amidst the staircases. As if I was moving around a magic spell. Ultimately, I stopped and pricked my ears. From a distance, shouts and laughter of children could be heard. It was possible for me to avoid Pinki Salman. Now probably, the game had changed. I had become valuable for him, just like a rat for a cat that plays before putting it in its mouth.

What you thought to be a staircase was actually you, the voice of Pinki Salman sailed in. A child cannot determine the time and place of his birth. Similarly, a boy cannot refuse the kind of life laid down for him.

Was Pinki Salman's relationship not restricted to the marriage register? Was the veil over his life related to something else? He who faced the sea dragon. Did he restrict himself to filling up the columns of the register because of bribes and packets of sweets? I surveyed the stairs with new hopes. I found myself in every staircase like a seven-year-old, eyes curious and heart scared of the unseen world. The next moment I was transformed into a 17-year-old Chinese boy, present on every stair from one end to the other. He was also there amongst the haze of the steps at both ends, watching me with dim eyes.

See, Pinki Salman's voice came in. What you have lost by coming into existence. But the voice was weird, as if a seven-year-old child, a 17-year-old boy, and a 70-year-old man were speaking simultaneously. You see what you want to see, and likewise, inside the bioscope, your picture turns hazy. Worms devour them and then nothing remains. I have to reply to lakhs of people on the Day of Judgement. This will go on through generations. My sins follow me till the Day of Judgement. I should not have disembarked from the ship. Probably, escaping from the jaws of the dragon proved to be the cause of my failure.

After this, I did not hear Pinki Salman's voice. It was possible that he was standing close to me and had become hollow from the inside. It was also possible that there was no difference between his presence and absence, as in Puranic stories, where absence and presence are the same.

***

The marriage register is standing on the rails of the window. I am trying to come out of it. Though I have succeeded in bringing both my hands out of the register, there was nothing to hold on to except the air. My skull, till the forehead, has come out. The pages are flapping on my face. My eyes can see rupa fish swimming in curved holes. They are coming out from the pages, crawling on my stomach, intestines and entering my ears. I can see the ink-soaked pages fast turning into dust; its stink impossible for me to bear. I accelerate my attempts to come out of the register. Before the register turns into dust and buries me forever, I have to come out of it.

I must come out of the register!

I must come out of the register!

I must come out of the register!

***

ARRIVAL

MAHMOUD YASIEN

In my childhood, I used to stare at it for hours with bewildered eyes and surprised looks. For me, in those days, its presence was baffling and confusing. I would gaze at it for a long time amidst the void of the universe, my curious and searching eyes steadfastly trying to explore its mystifying existence.

Then one day, when I was walking on the street of my *mohalla*—which goes straight from the west to the east, and ends up near a pathway close to the park used by the locals for strolling and pleasure in the evening—my yearning reached its peak. I knew that walking straight up the pathway, and on the other side of the park, I would be so close that with a little sprint I could catch up with it.

On the eastern side of this straight path, a triangular shape was formed in such a way that in between the park and the pathway, or opposite to it, another road—as far as the eye could see—ran from the north to the south. The park had beautiful iron railings on all sides, which, after every five or seven feet, were fastened to two-square-feet broad pillars built upon two-

and-a-half or three-feet-tall and quarter-feet-broad walls. The walls were strong, cemented, and the light green paint on the railings could still be seen. As far as the eye could see, the park was covered with green turf, the arrangements of lights within undertaken with care. It was probably done for the sake of creating a space for the public to walk. Amid the park was an island-like structure meant for rest and respite. The stairs and the sitting spaces were cast in cement, the insides of which were moulded in iron. The park was considerably large and spacious. It was three-quarter furlongs long (from the south to the north) and half a furlong wide (from the west to the east). There was a main gate flanked by two smaller ones on both sides and joined together with iron railings.

Where the width of the park ended, the straight path again went on its way, and at the eastern end (that is, at the far end) it merged into the pavement which was the starting point of another *mohalla*. A narrow lane from the edge of the pavement led to a desolate masjid, its minaret visible from a far distance. My target was to walk on this street and reach there, for according to my estimate, it was possible for me to arrive at it from this point.

The wider end of the park was in fact its last point. The street acted as its subway and merged with the park to form another starting point. Two streets ran parallel to each other from the south, intersecting each other till they reached the northern side. (It was on these that cars whizzed past). In between there was also a pavement that divided them into two, though intermittently leaving gaps of 10 to 15 feet that acted like subways to let the fast cars pass through and catch up with other lanes. This straight street ran through one of the gaps.

I do not know why I had come this way (possibly to fetch rations for daily use) for at one end was a ration shop. The shop catered to the needs of the public, supplying the nearby areas with weekly rations. If the government, with the introduction of the system of ration cards, had eased some lives by supplying items of daily use, it created unrest for the deprived and lesser-income groups which failed to understand the complicated ration-card system. This system proved to be a boon for men with a nose for business. They knew how to earn money by selling ration items in the black market. Thus, the fake ration cards far outweighed the original card holders (most of them made by the ration shop owners themselves for their personal benefits).

From the street and the park, on the other end of the pavement, I could see it from close quarters. It seemed stuck to the masjid's minaret. In my heart of hearts, I was exhilarated. I was capable of reaching it somehow. It was possible to get a hold of it. (It could not move away from there, or that is what I thought.) But in the meantime, I forgot what items I had come to purchase. The thoughts of home eluded me, even the fear of my father. (In my childhood, I was scared of my father who would beat me to his heart's content for the smallest of my faults). In those days, I would neglect my studies, being more interested in sports and games. It was possible that this pursuit could be psychologically related to my interest in fooling around.

For so long this object had struck me with awe and surprise. In my heart, I had always wanted to be close to it. Whenever I had the chance to climb the rooftop of any house, my eyes would gawk at it. I remember once visiting the house of my friend, Sagar, for the purpose of flying kites on the terrace of his four-storeyed building. Extending half my body from the cornice of the terrace, and like a swan protruding my neck, I gazed intently at it for a long time. But as before, it remained out of my reach. I even tried to look at it from the roof of our house, perched perilously on the highest point of the water tank, with extreme caution (to avoid tumbling down) so that it may come within my grasp. But I got scared and the distance between us became even greater.

Today, walking on this path, an inexpressible feeling was overpowering me. My unfulfilled wish was going to be realised. With these thoughts I entered the park through one of the smaller entrances. With confident steps I reached the eastern end of the park and its eastern gate. Crossing the park, I arrived at the pathway that led to the pavement. It seemed the pathway had helplessly moved to the north–south direction since it had no other option.

To cut the story short, I reached the last pavement without losing sight of it. Then with a panting heart and soft steps, I entered the lane. I was scared that it may give me the slip as on previous occasions and take refuge somewhere else. I regret to say, that arriving there, I understood I had made a wrong assessment. That one can make a wrong assessment of anything from afar had never occurred to me before. As it is, childhood days are bereft of such ideas. Still, just to satisfy myself, I thought it prudent to inch forward and went even beyond the masjid. My curious eyes were constantly in its pursuit. At one point it seemed close, almost merging into the ground. But when I stared at the tall building on my right side, my heart gave in. It was far and even beyond the tall building. (The existence of the building made me conscious of it; otherwise, it seemed as if it was still stuck to the terrace.)

Then with a broken heart I smothered my wish to stare, touch or grasp it. This yearning of mine was another name of something that remains unfulfilled forever.

MR STORAGE

MAHMOUD YASIEN

Mr Storage—I met him last night in my dreams. He was a sad man. He was bent under the unbearable debt that was pulling him down. His house, furniture, and other things, had been pawned in his native country. God knows since when? And his wife, children! Ah! I made a blunder. I failed to enquire about them. Actually, in my dream, it just escaped me; otherwise, I would have enquired. God knows how they might be passing their time! Mr Storage must have left them behind in his native country and ventured out to earn something. Now I can remember that he had taken a small shop on rent with his savings, for some years, on a contractual basis, about which I do not know much at this moment. It was also possible that the shop might have been taken on rent by someone else, and I had attributed it to him (you are right, my memory in real life is short). This can be possible for, in my dream, I had also met other people and moved with them, just as in real life when we come across one another. There were also men from the army whose behaviour was rude, just like personnel in real life from the army and the police who have no respect for the weak and misuse their power and position. I remember properly (for I never forget people who commit atrocities on me; the feeling of vengeance never makes me forget them) a tall, stout army man who (I don't remember the occasion) was given the responsibility of manning the gate. In my dream, he not only insulted me by not allowing me to enter the gate, but also a middle-aged woman (it is possible that the woman may be aged, I don't remember) rudely, grabbing her by her clothes and throwing her out of the gate. Even in my dream, I wanted to quarrel with him but desisted, taking into consideration my weakness and inherent vulnerability.

Mr Storage tried to decorate and spruce up the shop he had taken on rent for some years according to his extraordinary abilities and business acumen. The original owner, who was possibly close by, said excitedly that if he placed so and so items in particular showcases, they would look good. Mr Storage protested saying that cannot be done. The man cannot derive benefits from the shop till the contract period was over. Mr Storage looked very angry. Since I was present there, and by then, in the dream, I had developed enough intimacy with Mr Storage, I started speaking in his favour. I don't know whether the owner was satisfied or not—anyway, Mr Storage and I again became involved in interesting conversation. It was then I came to know that Mr Storage was a good novelist. He used to write in English. I think I might have either seen or read his novels. (How can one remember exactly the events of dreams?) Then it happened that with intense feeling, he expressed his willingness to earn something extra which, with the second publication of his novel, he failed to do. It might be copyright hurdles, or something else, so immediately, I expressed my opinion: 'I will translate your novel in my mother tongue.'

He looked stunned and stared at me.

'Yes! I want to translate your novel. I write short stories and articles in my mother tongue. I also translate interesting writings. They are appreciated by publishers.' I looked at his face with expectation. For a moment, he stared at me with a lost look. Then, he extended his right hand and gripped mine with delight (the way people usually shake hands to express jubilation) as if the permission for translation had been granted. I, too, to express my joy, shook his right hand two or three times. This was my expression of acceptance.

Then perhaps a discussion went on about payments and commissions. He was lenient here (no matter a great writer like him was bowed down with debt). We were discussing these nitty-gritties when Mr Storage, I do not know why, kept for himself a meagre amount of the commission. I do not know why I said: 'I suppose you are forgetting some provisions related to the commission. At least half the amount should be yours, and you are allotting more than half to me.'

Probably, he understood the point. I do not know what else was the subject of discussion in the dream—I just remember that his part of allotment was two lakhs, which instead of uplifting his spirits, made him feel lost and sad. 'What's the matter?' I asked him quietly. 'Are you not satisfied with the amount?'

He spoke in a heavy voice: 'What am I to do with these two lakhs? My house and furniture are lying pawned in Germany.'

Probably he might have said something more; I do not recollect. Anyway, the anguish on his face, voice, or the restlessness in his speech, distressed me. In order to console him I said: 'Alright, let us do this. You take two and a half lakh rupees.' (I kept only 50,000 for myself. I was confident that I would be able to carry on with this amount—only in a dream). Still, I could easily see that cheerfulness had not returned to his face. God knows how many pawned items he wanted to retrieve with the amount? What other wishes he had to fulfil? It was possible he may have unmarried daughters to be married off, making him pensive. But these thoughts did not occur in my dreams. There was no question about them. In dreams, people seek happiness, not sorrows of life.

In the end, I do not know why I told him with confidence: 'Okay, you take the full amount and free yourself from the entanglement of your present problem. You may return the amount of my commission later.' It was my sincerest desire to see him happy, at least on that occasion. He started chirping. (I wanted to see how a man despite his sorrows and sufferings could be happy … How he could smile regardless of the tears in his eyes.) Still, he, like a milk-sucking kid, failed to smile. It really pained me. In the end, my voice also cracked. I tried to control myself and, in my characteristic way, with all my sympathy intact, sadly said: 'You tell me, what more can I do to ease your problem? Why don't you return to your native country?'

He replied: 'Money is out here, not there.'

Both of us became reflective. Perhaps at that moment, we were standing face to face on some pavement, or lying on the grass, close to one another. I cannot properly recollect. Then we left the place with marks of sadness on our faces. The thought never occurred to me in my dream that he might have written another novel, and the same amount could easily have come with its translation too. I woke up at that moment, and felt sad, for I never wanted to part with him. I wanted to remain close and share his grief. I wanted to free him from his sorrows.

Now (early in the morning), perched on my bed, with papers on my lap, a pen in hand, I am trying to turn the dream into a story.

A HALF-SERIOUS STORY

MAHMOUD YASIEN

And then walking by his side, I suddenly turned into an old man (I had gone to see him off). Moments earlier, my friend who came to meet me—probably he had returned after appearing at a competitive examination somewhere—said something (he had expressed his opinion about life in such a way) when we were having tea sitting in a small café in the *mohalla*, talking about some problems of life, (he) seriously/(I) semi-seriously participating in the discussion (that is, he was serious and I was half serious). During the discussion he suddenly asked me about the length of time it took me to come from non-existence into existence, I hesitatingly, falteringly said: '19 days!'[1] He took the passage of 19 moments of my life as 19 centuries and started moralising, giving important advice about the remaining part of life.

He had another friend with him—someone called Roshan Ali—and I had also taken him along into the café.

---

1 Now the passage of time had made it into 59 (Time's merciless slaughter of innocent four decades).

During the discussion, my friend clarified his advice further, and I went on getting lost in his conversation, but I had not forgotten my present state of affairs—I had not forsaken the reality of my existence. Rather, I was fast contemplating the past and the future. My thoughts were failing me. Sometimes it made me anxious; at others, my head reclined with the burden of thoughts. My friend was artless and inexperienced. He could not listen to what went inside my mind. He failed to read the inner portion of myself.

When I came out of the café, customarily offering him cigarettes and betel leaves (which he willingly accepted, except for his friend who was not addicted to these), even at that time, I was young.

We talked as we trudged along—his counselling went on, and I half-heartedly went on with yes, yes. Deep within, I was feeling penitent, and together with remorse, the light of reason from the region of the subconscious to the conscious was becoming visible at the levels of perception.

I was on my way to see them off.

When I looked at myself in the light of his counsels, and with the eye of imagination analysed my existence (physically) and by a self-analysis, and then (for myself) examined objectively the lives of famous personalities on levels of existence and non-existence—and weighed them on the scales of reason, then it was as if all my hopes were dashed to pieces. It was then—walking the paths, suddenly—as a matter of habit, looking at the broad, square mirror on a small *paan* and cigarette shop (I saw my face) and suddenly felt like an old man—an inexperienced old man totally untested of the experiences of life (I was deeply affected by the events: Was this the life that we consciously and/or unconsciously tried to lead with passionate intensity?)

Suddenly, the overcast sky filled the world with its downpour, and cold rain dropped on our bodies. I desisted from moving forward, apologised to both, shook hands, said 'Khuda Hafiz' and hurriedly left.

I was running all the way till I reached home. I found myself young again—and had completely forgotten the words of my friends.

I do not have the habit of forgetting. But I know this much; in this vast ocean, lakhs of people like me search, crores are in the quest, but instead of swimming are just moving their hands and feet: so what's the significance of a drop in the ocean? I had to feign an act of forgetfulness! (When the search is futile and the conditions unfavourable, what else can be done?)

All this can be my immaturity!

PSYCHE

MAHMOUD YASIEN

We are a psychic process which we do not control, or only partly direct. Consequently, we cannot have any final judgment about ourselves or our lives. If we had, we would know everything but at most that is only a pretence. At bottom we never know how it has all come about. The story of a life begins somewhere, at some particular point we happen to remember; and even then it was already highly complex. We do not know how life is going to turn out. Therefore, the story has no beginning, and the end can only be vaguely hinted at.

—C.G. Jung, *Memories, Dreams, Reflections*

I am on board an *ekka*. Maybe in place of the coachman, or by his side, or inside it, sitting on the back seat and the carriage is moving as if on wings. Suddenly, it happens that a deep gorge appears out of nowhere, on both sides of which there is a bridge made of rope and wood, or wood and rope. The carriage, which is drawn by stout horses, moves swiftly along the bridge. Then, I do not know how, we, I mean the coachman and me, together with the *ekka*, enter some *mohalla*, where there are huts that look like houses or houses like huts. Some are battered and burnt, while others are in good shape. Some seem to have no roofs. From the houses or doors of the huts, windows, and doorsteps, people stare at us (it seems so to me). Someone continuously whispers in my ears (it may be the voice from the other side of the world or the words of the coachman).

"This is the abode of the dead (And all who peek out are dead)."

My neck, together with my eyes, too, mechanically stare at them in bewilderment. The vehicle is moving fast and covering the stretch while I keep on staring. I see somebody from the front side, when the *ekka* moves by them, and others I turn to look back, when the carriage has moved away from them (at an even pace). They are, in fact, motionless and unmoved, without blinking an eye, and without moving their necks, they continuously gawk at a single spot. Women, men, children, and the old, all gaze towards us or which way do they? But they stare towards the road from both sides of the houses, protruding out their necks like swans. Some of their necks are stretched, stiff like stones, others drooping as if blood had dried in them or had been squeezed out. Then suddenly, I do not know how, from the front side, a solemn, angry-looking face, with wide eyes, open-mouthed, edges fast towards me (Or maybe the face was still and the *ekka* was fast being drawn towards it). Bewildered and distraught, I shriek in a heart-rending voice. But my voice gets choked inside my throat. Then what happens is that crossing the dirty *nullah*, I happen to clearly see from the carriage, fresh and long grasses, drenched with water (I do not know whether from rain or the dark, dirty water from the descending *nullah*). Anyway, someone again whispers in my ears (May be the coachman might have said it using the whip on the horses, or not using it, but only tugging at the reins [so that the horses may stop there] and turned around to address me): "We have come the wrong way. There is no way ahead."

Probably I babble and reply or reply and babble: "Now what is to be done?" (Probably scared of going back the way to the abode of the dead, say it meekly). My eyes are stuck on the stagnant or overflowing black filth of the *nullah*. I get the reply: "We have to turn back the *ekka* and cover the same stretch again." Then whether the carriage turned back or not! Anyway, I find myself inside the New Market, near a tea stall, where there is a small crowd of people. I find some coins still safely ensconced in my pocket. I also order a cup of tea for myself. People are whispering amongst themselves. They are speaking in soft voices about the abode of the dead. I also try to agree with them and join to give assent to their conversation (as is the custom of ours). Probably I tell them that I have just come from the same place (Or probably they might have been talking about some serious mishap or accident, and I might have told them about my return from there). Then probably after having tea from the cup made of burnt earthenware, I place it in a corner, pay the price and return home.

I do not know whether the same day, while returning home after having tea, or some other day, long ago, or not very long, passing by the scary lane (this feeling—scary one, creepy feeling of the lane, of eeriness—belonged to my childhood or boyhood days), which goes to my house dissecting complex and criss-cross lanes, I meet, on the road on the other side, which is away from the normal way, and a turn before which I had to take, a woman, who had been spreading her thick, black, long hair scarily on her face and drawing the attention of the public for no reason at all and forcing them to become scared, all of a sudden. I also become highly petrified. As and when my eyes fall on this sinister woman (my hairs stand on ends, my voice falters) I recite some Quranic verses to ward off my fear: probably *Surah-e Fatiha/Naas/ Falaq/Ikhlas/Ayaat ul Kursi* (or whatever, I do not remember). When satisfaction does not come from it, then I sing, though the voice seems to be subdued, some songs, in an odd way, or you can say that in a subdued voice I shriek as I sing. (But in my heart the recitation of the Quranic verses goes on [the net result was I remained stuck between the Quranic verses and the tune of the song]). Then what happens is that on another turn lies a lane coming from the opposite direction, which away from the normal route, on the other side, comes out of a main entrance of a house. A snake charmer or a magician appears out of nowhere playing soothing music on a flute and I, as if swooning and charmed, start swinging to the melodious tune. Yet, the hurry to reach home also continuously seems to lead my steps towards my home. So much so that in such a state (that is walking in a trance like state) I cross that junction too and then arriving at another junction, where, according to me, the danger seems to be over, I flutteringly turn around and fall down (My legs get entangled with some unknown object lying on the ground).

Then one day, probably that same day, the same night—someone, I do not know why, stabs me (in my stomach or chest with a sharp dagger) and I, because of the fear or fright of death, with a stifled shriek, fall to the ground (I feel extremely sorry for my untimely death [Why did someone kill me for no reason? What have I done to anybody?] Together with it I also think [if I am dead then I should have been totally motionless and lifeless: why these thoughts and worry?]. Now who will be able to apprehend my murderer? For only I know him; because I had seen him push the dagger into my stomach/chest. [Who will believe it was him that killed me? Who will be able to reach him without my giving witness?] I don't know how I become motionless and lifeless and how I suddenly regained consciousness. With nervousness I quickly look all around myself: I don't find anything around. Suddenly my hand, right or left, or maybe both, instinctively move towards my navel. There is no gash in my stomach [I try to feel it]. There is no feeling of pain or pricking sensation: the respiratory system is working in its usual way. I only feel the heart beating faster. I heave a sigh of relief [I am happy I am alive. I thank God]).

Then one day, as I stare at the roof of the bedroom, I am shocked. A very ugly (scary) black, fat-bodied snake is slithering along. It is trying to coil itself with the bamboo and wood and I do not know how mysteriously it is twisting itself over the main door, sometimes hiding, and at others, coming out at the other end as it is moving along. The constant rubbing of its body with the pillar and beam or ridgepole does not create any noise, nor does it make any hissing sound (vicious enemy). It is trying to slither away quietly to some unknown destination or maybe trying to find a suitable place from where to attack its prey. Though I am scared, yet I do not know from where such strength comes to me, that instead of running away, I stand steadfast trying to find some way of escape out of it (Maybe, I might have been worried about the fate of my two sisters who were fast asleep, either on the mat on the floor or on the camp cot. Or maybe, one on the mat and the other on the cot, or both together or away from each other: I mean in two different places, or maybe it was only one sister, the other somewhere else [That is, at their elder sister's house]). The snake is not bothered about me (it is possible that it might have kept me under its watch, or another reason may be that I might not have got the chance of escape from the room!), crazily engaged in its intoxicated meanderings. It is busy winding itself against the door of the main entrance, pillar, bamboo or pole and its slithering kind of movement. Wherever it finds an opening, a hole, or a space to come out, it sticks out its head, and before long comes out at another spot. Its vicious ways made it difficult for me to ascertain its exact length. But at different spots, bamboo, ridgepole or pillar, the coating, or the windings of its body, could certainly give some idea of its length, which was like the span of the intestines associated with the devil. Then what happens is that it tosses itself to dangle below, and, sticking close to the protruding parts of the bed, it starts descending (Then, before batting an eyelid, I do not know how, it suddenly comes down).

Now, since it has completely descended to the floor, its mobility and movements seemed to have developed a bizarre manner of approach. In a twinkling of an eye, it disappears from a spot and appears at another that is almost close to me, with its magnificence and I have to show enormous alertness on my part. I am surprised as to what has happened to its length when it was above? Further, I am surprised at my own steadfastness that suddenly develops in me. I am more worried and scared about my sisters (or one sister) causing worry and afflicting me, because of urgency, or failure of apprehension, I had failed to tell them to be cautious (God forbid! Supposing I had woken them up then it was possible that the snake might have proceeded towards them). The snake is making its attempt on me and closely attacking me, and with each attack, a kind of a tempest emits from its mouth and within a twinkling of an eye gets lost in the dim darkness of the room. I, anyway, do not know how I, despite its quickness and ferocity, am able to finish it off. (It could not, to me or my sisters [or one sister] do any harm. Though time and again, it had passed by my sisters or around them with slithering movements. It has also made an attempt to attack me, with all its fiery and poisonous ways. But thank God! Whether this way or that, it failed to do them any harm). Outside, it seems dawn has descended and a faint, diffused, soft and velvety sunlight filters through the doors and windows: the night lamp is switched off.

Then again, one day, possibly after a long time, my eyes are glued to the sky and I see a gathering of bloodshot knitted clouds—just like carding fluffy cotton but extremely red; traits of blood in it, and with overflowing intensity, coming towards me. I, comprehending a bit, or not understanding a little, to my right side, or somewhere close, address a man by pointing to him the bloodshot clouds. He, too, looks at me surprised and then stares at the overflowing blood-drenched clouds (I do not know what calamity is going to fall? We tell ourselves in our hearts and then express our opinions). Then I direct my eyes to the right side of the sky (probably trying to see how far is the stretch of the cloud?). But on this side, the sky appears to me totally blue and clear as if nothing had taken place. Likewise, one day, I do not know how long, on the western side, I find hailstorm falling from the sky: balls of fire, small and big; parts of embers, big and small. Then a miracle happened, I do not know what came to mind, I lifted up both my hands for *dua*, as an act of supplication. I had also closed my eyes; whether moved with emotion or thinking that it may add a sense of devotion (which is appreciated by God) and then after a while, when I opened my eyes I saw, as far as my eyes could survey, blue and clear, smiling firmament. One or two stars were also shining with unmatched brilliance, their reflections penetrating straight into my eyes. Then, from the main entrance from which I had been witnessing the miracle, I stepped out to see the situation outside. Everything there was all right. But when I ventured out to the big *maidan*, where, on one pretext or the other I always go, I found piles of burnt bricks spread all over as if balls of fire from the sky had fallen and cooled down there. The roof of the island structure, situated in the middle, also had burnt bricks, small and big pieces spread all over.

I also remember the stupidity of my childhood when one day (or it may be possible when I had grown up but my childish behaviour still remained dominant) in my family house (do not know which one: where I was born? Or where I had spent the earlier part of my childhood? Or where I am living now?) catching the pipe of the wall close to the main entrance, I climbed up like a monkey, and, stuck out my neck from the rooftop, boastfully shouting so that my voice could travel to another corner. I used my full lung power and shouted:

"Hey, you *bhoot*!"

There was no reply.

"Hey, you bloody *bhoot*!"

After a while, totally unexpectedly, a voice came from afar, of a weird kind; trapped, indistinct, and soft:

"Yea! I am coming—!"

And it seems my body shivered, feelings turned into smoke; hands and feet became numb. I do not know how, in a state of bewilderment, I quickly managed to come down.

EPIC OF THE NEW COLONY

MAHMOUD YASIEN

If there are any souls in Hell, it is not because they have been sent there, but because Hell is where they insist upon being.

—W.H. Auden

1

Four anti-socials have given us a hard time. They are extraordinarily united, strong, and beyond reach. They harass, instil fear, and continuously change strategies to belittle us.

They belong to an infamous club of the *basti*.[1] The club controls everything and is the centre of anti-social activities. Their aim is to drive us away from our ancestral homes and they focus their might on infringing upon our liberty.

The club fully controls the municipal corporation, the local MLA, MP, panchayat, zilla pradhan, police, and different courts. What about the denizens of the colony? Their position is restricted to being the audience, dance according to their tunes, or like dogs, wag tails in front of the members.

1 Writer's note: This *basti* is actually a huge colony like the United States of America, which was once a colony of Great Britain. You may call it 'A World in Miniature'.

The club members' behaviour towards us is worse than beating or throwing us out of our houses or flinging away our furniture. It is sad and worthy of condemnation. It is not only restricted to this; anyone who speaks in our favour on moral or humanitarian grounds, or for brotherhood's sake, or tries to strengthen any kind of relationship is tormented in ways that they think it safe to remain quiet. This is how the club members have encircled us from all sides, making us vulnerable and helpless. We have become fully captive.

The club members think that it is their birthright to poke their noses into every work of the colony, be it a marriage, religious festivals, or sad occasions like death. Everything depends on their whims. Their order must be adhered to otherwise, the consequences would follow. People acquiesce to remain out of harm's way. Only one odd man remains their target of attack, the focus of their might and muscle.

The cause of the enmity between us was the tussle between ruffians and gentlefolks. It is a century-old story of conflict, the narration of which would be tantamount to raising dead issues. It leads to nowhere. To cut a long story short, in such a violent struggle, the ruffians suffered a humiliating defeat, the burden of insult and ignominy which they now carry on their shoulders. It is from that point onwards that the generations of hooligans, gangsters, and thieves created a united front and a sinister intrigue against us.

The habits of us gentlefolks are to keep things confined to ourselves. We are not bothered about others. Thus, knowing our weaknesses and disunity, these offspring of anti-socials made life hell for us, and they harass our family members on the streets. When we protest, they hurt us in numerous ways. If we keep on with the protests, they do not hesitate to kill. They have decimated our leaders. None in our family can seriously think about the problem, find a solution, or discover ways to bring us out of this quagmire.

Experience tells us that the club members are playing the same game that the united forces played with Germany and Japan during World War II. They spread new propaganda against us in order to wipe out the last trace of sympathy that might have been left in the public.

The continuous sufferings have robbed us of vigour; our energy sagged, and we have become hopeless. We rely on fate. But things have not stopped here. With this cowardice, life's problems have accelerated: racial annihilation and the question of survival stare at us starkly. We stand face to face with a serious ordeal of life.

We are members of a united family; one family is related to innumerable members who walk the way of life together. Each has his individual and united ways of facing life's challenges and solving problems in characteristic ways. Who does not love his wife, children, and parents? Who does not admire their siblings or have regards for the elders? Thus, every individual of our family in domestic life is extremely sensitive. They do not want to see the members of their family pestered, insulted, or die before their time. Yet they remain separated from each other, at times, irresponsibly, even though they do not wish it to be so. They act as if nothing will take place in the future to insult, provoke or finish us off.

The irony is we are fully aware of these. Each and every member of our family knows how we are caught in the accursed net. We face it mechanically and remain devoid of responsibilities and duties, except for a few simple-minded youths, whose number is negligible, that remain rebel and radical. It is expected that these few would not give in but offer a decent fight and, if need be, prove that they who think are monarchs of the time are actually cowards. It is expected that these youths would be able to influence the people and win them over.

I have tried to clarify before them with examples that the apparently small number of anti-socials have the backing of the whole colony. Besides, they exercise power because of the timidity of the colony, the blind acceptance of their demands and the welcome they give to their actions. The public has become submissive and scared. They are, in fact, more chicken-hearted than us. So how can they become our saviours? Now we are forced to accept that even the colony's citizens are in favour of the atrocities committed against us—in their hearts, they wish we remain oppressed and subjugated forever.

One day, one of my daughters, who was a student of journalism at the university, was surrounded by some unruly students. They were from some political party. They started teasing her. When things crossed the limits, she, who was well versed in karate, tried to defend herself. She gave the assaulters two or three karate knocks on their thighs, ribs, and behind the ears. The attack was serious. Firstly, they were shocked; then, like wild dogs, they pounced on her, and in no time, managed to overpower her. Then what those predators did publicly, a father cannot describe in words. Those wicked people filmed the whole episode on their video camera. The passers-by watched the event either due to fear or curiosity. This always happens when a few, to satisfy their lust, have always succeeded because others remained mute spectators.

I do not know how my daughter managed to reach home. But when she did, there was a hue and cry. We helplessly shed silent tears. What else could we do? Remaining mute and suffering silently had been our ways for centuries.

We also faced another setback as the local police refused to file even a general diary. They detained us for hours, asking irrelevant questions. In the meantime, the police officer got constant calls, and silently whispers poured into the receiver. Possibly he was seeking advice from some important personage. Ultimately, he agreed to file the diary. Hours passed, after which the officer-in-charge deputed a flying squad with a sergeant and a few constables. The officer sat in a red-coloured jeep. We went along. But the police, instead of visiting the area of the crime, interrogated, intimidated, and made us feel scared.

The condition at the university was calm. There was no protest from any quarters. The vice-chancellor and the president of the student's union refused to acknowledge the involvement of any student of the institution. They said that the accusation was baseless. The opposition party of the students' wing also kept mum. Since the episode had taken place outside the university campus, they said that no one from the institution could be held accountable.

So, nothing fruitful came out of our attempts. People at home remained hopeless; my wife wailed, and my daughter! She had turned into a stone. She kept on staring into nothingness. God only knows what? She had forgotten to express her feelings.

Wherever we went for her medical check-up, we were ignored. The same excuse of being engaged was given everywhere. We became hopeless. After a long search, a good-natured gynaecologist finally agreed to visit our house. But because of the interference of the club members, he was forced to return. The anti-socials on motorbikes surrounded our car from all sides and started peeping inside with ill intentions. The gynaecologist became so scared that he immediately got out of the vehicle. We sat helplessly and watched. Fear and terror were mixed with affront and vulnerability. The ruffians did not tarry, and instead moved their bikes and disappeared.

3

They had, till now, only targeted our education, jobs, and population. But another item was added to their agenda. Now they wanted to attack our culture. In order to belittle us, they spread propaganda in every locality so that our heads would bow down with shame in the colony. They must have taken this step keeping in mind the importance of culture, its permanence, and the way it exercised justice and fair play. They must have undertaken intensive study before taking such a step.

The terrible way in which my daughter was treated, her video made, was an attack on our culture. It lowered our dignity. It was like throwing acid on the face of our culture, reducing it within minutes to nothingness. They had destroyed everything in that short time. We were not ready for such low treatment from them.

Before this, the club members had not dared to touch our women or had shown any inclination to attempt such an act. It was possible that they must have been scared of public opinion or the colony's wrath. But the colony remained unaffected and quiet. Before the arrival of the club members, the condition was good, untainted, and conducive. The people, irrespective of caste or creed, were so closely knit that even blood relationships or kinship had no meaning. But the hooligans, in order to cast their net, spread the poison of communalism and hatred in such a way that the whole area was impacted. The society and culture crumbled. (Who knows how many centuries may be needed to wipe out its effect, to find a solution? Or whether it would ever come out of its labyrinth?)

Things had crossed all limits. Now in order to survive, it was necessary to fight back. This was the only way left for survival. We called an emergency meeting in the hall of our ancestral home in which the selected family members participated enthusiastically. Most of them were youths who were serious and practical. Amongst them were also youths known for their rebellious way of life. In a way, they guided the meeting and were spirited entities. With the seriousness of attitude and sincerity of approach laden on their shoulders, they were ready to take the hooligans and shake the colony from the ins and outs.

But the elders who had experienced the vicissitudes of life advised them to arrive at a compromise as well as refrain from taking any decision in haste or with anger so that the matter may not become complicated or take an ugly turn. Especially after my daughter's barbaric incident, they believed that any humane treatment from the club members should not be expected. Now that we were openly at arms, our steps must be cautious. The club members naturally will not take it lying low.

The youths believed that whether we took cautious steps or came out in the open, the club members would not sit idle. Their aim was our destruction. The proposal of the youths was an all-out attack with such intensity that the club members may not get time to fight back. We will, they said, do it taking a risk on a do-or-die basis, for one must remember the words of God: 'They who die in self-defence will be martyrs.'

We were still in the midst of the discussion when, either from the roof or window passage, something fell on the floor. It was a paper tied to a stone. From the written note, we were intimated that the club members had been aware of our meeting and, to counter our attacks, a truck full of men with hockey sticks, cricket bats, *lathi*s, as well as soda bottles and bombs, were on the way towards the colony.

4

The information made us sad. A sudden calamity had befallen us. We were planning for an attack but now we had to defend ourselves. No immediate solution came our way. We were at a loss: there was no idea of the timing and manner of their imminent attack. Now we had to be more alert than before. The first act was to bolt and fasten each door and window and pull down heavy curtains so that light may not be visible from the outside. This was how we could once again easily reschedule our plan of defence.

The children were hurdled to the safety of the inner rooms, and women and girls with them so that if an attack made the children wail, the women folks could take care of them. We could be rest assured on that count. After that, we took positions by stationing ourselves against the doors and windows; armed with kitchen knives, scissors, stilettos, and broken pieces of wood: an example of a drowning man grasping at straws.

They would regularly plan attacks, create disturbances, and fracas as a strategy to weaken us. After enkindling the fire of arson and violence, they would douse it by proclaiming the return of peace in the area. But this would be an excuse to enter each house and search every household. (The club members would do this with the help of their so-called social workers, who were on their payrolls, members of Inter Bustee Amnesty, and Brotherhood Rights.) After the destruction by the club members, these men, in different guises of peace and brotherhood, would perform the duties of combing up operations, taking away whatever things we had in our homes.

There was the noise of the movement of a heavy lorry or truck, the gurgling sound of the engine, a sign of its slowing down. To my estimate, it must have stopped near my house. The hooligans started jumping down the truck, one by one. The clash of hockey sticks and *lathi*s, and the sound of bottles clanging together, sailed through the air. Probably these arsenals were being unloaded from the truck. We held on to our breaths, heartbeats increasing alarmingly. Anything could happen!

There was a sudden blast, and the whole area seemed to shake. My heart jumped up in fear. It seemed like a lot could occur within a fraction of a minute. The noise must have come from a bit of a distance. The bomb could have accidentally exploded, falling off someone's hands. A din was heard, and there seemed to be a mad rush of feet. It was possible that some hands or feet had been blown off. We were caught in a dilemma of sorts: unable to see, we were just imagining things. We could not help doing so. In a way, it was allowing us time to gauge the developing situation, and on the other, making us ready for any eventuality.

We were still locked in the tense moment when suddenly, it seemed an earthquake struck our house. The doors and windows were hammered with *lathi*s and hockey sticks; glass window panes broke into pieces, and door latches crumbled. We sat cowed down, leaning against the walls. Our grips on our household weapons tightened. They started pelting stones that fell like showers and bottles rained on walls and closed doors. A bottle passed through the crack of the glass window and sailed to the hall before dashing against the wall, breaking into pieces, and scattering all over. My heart gave in. Several bombs were hurled simultaneously against the walls and rooftops. Other sounds of blasts were heard, disorientating us, our ears numb. It seemed that the whole building would crumble in a moment. The plaster of the walls came out in chunks at places and fell with a thud. We managed to survive by a whisker. Our heartbeats had increased, our throats were parched, and we were swallowing phlegm instinctively. Our bodies were also shivering and hands trembling as if we were on our last pins.

The wailings and shouting of women and children came from the inner room. We were caught in a dilemma of sorts, helpless and worried. Another round of blasts shook the area; another chunk of peeled plaster from the walls fell somewhere with a thundering sound. We had been badly caught in their net.

Still, we were ready to face them on a one-to-one basis because there was no way out. Earlier, as a caution, we had removed some falling-apart doors. Now we took in our hands the disentangled wood of those doors.

We were ready to face the enemy and so took positions against the doors. If someone dared to come in through the doors and the windows, we were ready to dispatch them to hell.

The wails and shouts of women and children had come to a stop. Now their tension had eased, and a sense of vengeance must have replaced their thoughts. The women took to boiling water in large cauldrons, and its hissing sound reached our ears.

Help for us was out of the question; helplessness and vulnerability now a part of ourselves. It was a new Mahabharat, a new Karbala for us. The whole colony was under its grip—helplessness and affront, a way of life.

5

We remained permanently locked up in the house. Every passing moment was telling on our nerves. Slowly, the desire for necessities came to an end. Our energies sagged, our bodies shrank, clothes loosened, and our hands became numb. It was now difficult to stand or even sit properly. We just sat on beds or charpoys with closed eyes, like lifeless entities, hands clasped and bowed heads. We were cut off from the outside world. The club members kept guard outside so that no individual could venture out, nor any food items or necessities sent inside. Whether it was day or night, they guarded us like dogs with protruded tongues, ever watchful for their provision—our flesh and bones.

It may be a year—or decades or even a century—that we had been kept imprisoned like this. The only difference between the previous treatment and the present was that earlier, we were harassed, and now we were imprisoned in our houses.

They had initially cut off all supply lines, including water, for a month. They wondered how our members remained in good health and survived. They even surmised whether some organisation was helping us surreptitiously with supplies of necessary goods. If such a power was secretly helping us, they would one day openly come out in our defence. Then the members can cast their net to catch hold of them.

Sometime earlier also, insults and affronts had been heaped upon us—a sad and barbaric storm that had left us stunned. The villainy and barbarism of the club members that started with a boil had now turned into a full-fledged volcano. Even the child born to my daughter was forcibly taken away by these people (I cannot call them demons for God does not want us to call people names). They might have planned to make the child stand up against us in the future. (It shows how bankrupt they are both physically and mentally).

We were always finding ways to erase the stamp of infamy on us. How do we do that? God seemed to have heard our prayers. It was also possible that the Creator used this to grant his innocent creation an exceptional place in his Grace, just like Moses, who was unknowingly granted safe haven by the pharaoh of the time.

6

This was the 17th day of our captivity. We had to spend 13 more days before it could end. Our present problems may end, but the question was, how do we spend these remaining days? How can we spend days which look like an impossibility? The water connection, together with phone and electricity, had been disconnected. Possibly they knew the importance of water. They might not have ruled out the possibility that we would be able to face them with renewed vigour when we came out of our captivity. Thus, the disconnection of water.

Our water reservoir, jars, buckets, jugs, mugs, everything was dry. Our throats were parched, our stomachs sagged; we had nothing to look up to. We had been reduced to nothing; weak and tired, exhaustion made us look drowsy, bodies limp as if with an attack of paralysis. It was then that I spotted my eight-year-old son. He had managed to find a piece of chalk from somewhere. Hunger made him chew it, maybe because of its smell. Soon he had it inside his mouth, but a strain of pain was visible on his face. The powdery grains might have gotten stuck in his throat. He started coughing relentlessly. I picked him up. He was now having hiccups. I thrust my fingers deep into his throat. His painful suffering wrenched my heart. My eyes were searching for something in the space, anything that could relieve him from the pain and satisfy the cravings of his hunger.

My sad eyes stared at my wife's breast that had shrivelled up. She quickly pulled her apparel and drew a part of it on her head. Then with a dawn of realisation, eyes shining, face aglow, she placed the child on her lap with his face towards her bosom. But disappointment returned to her face. She realised the condition of her dry self.

Helpless, but picking up lost energy, I trudged to the main door on weak legs to open the latch with shivering hands. (Now, I am not bothered about what punishment would be meted out to me by the club members if I violated their orders).

Suddenly through the half-ajar main door, a flash struck. I withdrew my head inside and closed the door. I stood close to it, out of breath. It was a bullet fired from a pistol or revolver fitted with a silencer. This meant that they wanted to annihilate us, freeing themselves from the mesh of legal tangles. Now they were not going to let us live. We had become a complete nuisance for them. With grief-stricken countenance and sad eyes, taking along the untold helplessness with me, I stared at the comatose individuals of our family. Now all escape routes had been cut off.

7

My son is lying unconscious on the lap of my wife. His eyes are dilated, he is breathing slowly, and again having hiccups. We are staring at each other with helpless eyes. We have lost the capacity for speech and hearing, and were sitting speechless. Our eyes speak; my family demands an answer from me through their eyes.

'What annoyed the club members that they held us ransom for so long? What don't they have? Knowledge, contacts, saviours, helpers spread all over … Compared to them, we remain alone, without any saviour.'

I try to calm the nerves of my family through my eyes.

'My beloved! These troubles are temporary. They guarantee you everlasting happiness and perpetual security. They prepare the fuels of hell for your enemies. These signify our victory and are symbols of their defeat.

'Some things are felt, they create images in our minds but we only disregard them. Other things happen before our eyes and we believe in their outer appearances. The reality is that we help create them, affected by our psyche.

'What we observe with our naked eye is a mirage. What remains invisible is the truth. In pain or anger, we rail at the Creator. Those words are, in reality, for our own selves. Complaints are made by cowards who have lost the capacity to fight against circumstances. Self-respecting individuals steer clear with hard work, reason, and sense of balance.'

Suddenly, my daughter, soft-spoken, quiet by nature, gets up as if from a trance. She snatches her brother from her mother's lap and goes to the other room with faltering steps.

We watch her with a sense of disbelief. But then our faces assume a sense of calm, anxiety mixed with fortitude.

We do not know what drama was being enacted with the rest of our family in other parts of the colony.

THE SHOP OF WORDS

SHAHIRA MASROOR

With the break of dawn, a truck stood before a closed shop. A man was bringing down things from the truck. It was difficult to know the contents as the sacks had been sealed. The man was not too old. He was standing on the threshold of the past and the future. His face was covered with a beard, cropped hair, and sharp eyes. He was oblivious to the surroundings. My curiosity gave me a nudge.

'What's your name?'

'Askari.'

Listening to the name, a century and another compressed itself as events appeared before my eyes. A green uniform and the pounding of black boots rushed onto the pages of the past.

'What is contained in these uncountable sacks?' I asked.

He turned around to look at me. He did not care about my question. Instead, he put a counter question to me.

'Will you tell me what kind of people live in and around here?'

'I have not got my answer,' I showed my impatience. 'You will come to know about them. But you did not tell me what is contained in these sacks?'

'You will soon come to know about the contents. I have come here for business purposes. I will stay for some time.'

Askari lifted the shutters of the shop. He requested passers-by to help him carry his belongings inside. I went on my way and, with the progress of the day, forgot the episode. But it was not obliterated. I had to face Askari every day, like I go through the daily newspaper, for his shop was near my house. Otherwise, scores of people like him appear in daily life; one business takes the form of another before getting buried under the debris of time. I was on the verge of forgetting when suddenly, one day, I saw Askari standing at the shop's threshold. The shop was old. It had not been cleaned properly; only the business was new. There was a flight of stairs leading to the door. The door and windows of the shop were open. His eyes were gazing at the dust coming from the street. His dress was just like ours, his identity through which he put his life at stake—on the flight, leaving home, jumping over walls, balls of fire dropping from the sun: 'What if we lose our identity? Take on a different guise ... But what's the benefit?' Even after performing all duties, we still remain strangers, for they had written it boldly, with burnt-out words: 'Whoever is born would remain like that. If you try to change your name, you get a bad name.'

It was impossible to remain mute and patient.

Many faces appeared—they who try to keep men imprisoned in cages. My thoughts, like the strings of kites, were getting unrolled by themselves.

Mr Askari gave my thoughts a shake. He wished me a *salaam* and addressed me:

'How are you? Hope you are fine. That day you didn't tell me your name. I didn't ask either.'

'What if you come to know my name? You do not even get lodging in the city with your real name.'

He came forward and put his hand on my shoulder.

'You are right. That is why this accident took place. They have completely obliterated our names. A lady who went to survey the area of the mishap returned in tears. The men accompanying her were also sad. Their statements filled up the columns of the newspapers. But that lady became dumb. The men with her, businessmen and unused to writing, are missing. The only one, who could have written about the accident, was that lady. Now the jute sacks of the lady are full of words. They are overflowing out of the sacks; train, fire, petrol, expectant woman, children, murder, camp, revenge. Now how much shall I recount; words that once shone now have lost their sheen. For a new accident, innumerable words have emerged.'

At the end of the speech, Askari's eyes were buried deep in their sockets. His cheekbones looked prominent.

'Mr Askari,' I said. 'Why are you weeping over spilt milk? I am impatient to know about you.'

'That is what I am telling you,' his eyes were full of tears. 'That day, you wanted to know about the contents of the sacks. During my life, on one pretext or the other, I have managed to gather up a large number of words. Now I have set up a shop. I want to do some business dealing with words. Don't you want to see my shop?'

Curiosity took hold of me. I crossed the flight of stairs and reached the door. Cobwebs had covered the room. The windows were still not properly opened. Inside the room, scents and odours, hopelessness, falsehood, truth, cause or no cause: heaps of words of these sorts had been piled up. Some passers-by may drop in, take a fistful of words or more, according to their taste. He may spread out hope and caution against the proliferation of darkness. Or he may not perform any of these. It is not mandatory. They who knit webs with words never face such a situation. Within me, I had started to play with words.

'Hello! What are you thinking? Shall I pack some words for you?'

'No, thanks, Mr Askari,' I was shaken. 'I am not used to weaving webs with words. Now is the time of moving pictures. Pictures that speak ...'

'*Wah* mister! What a statement! They do not have command over words. Those pictures move according to the wishes of someone. Can those pictures ever move according to your wishes? Never. They will make you wander over mountains at gunpoint. Travels over deserts amidst sandstorms or even stony floors may not be a hurdle for you. Click this. Take this. Don't ever arrest him … They may not stop here. They may even take you to their camps. Treat you with dignity. Water is unavailable in the desert. But they will treat you with the coolest beverages. On your return, one amongst them will take account of your exercise, destroy the pictures they don't like, make mute the words not to their liking. Do you understand?'

Listening to him, I felt infuriated. I tried to change the subject.

'Mr Askari, I will take some words from your repository. It would be like an inauguration of your shop. It will be the first step of my love for words.'

Askari turned around and picked some words from close quarters.

'Take them,' he said and started putting the words inside. On one hand was camp, missile, tank, Zionism, superpower, empire, and on the other, frenzy, impudence, suicide bomber …

'No,' I protested and pointed to the inner part of the shop, to the words under the debris of the passage of time, hanging from the cobwebs—tents, gardens, pastures, elephants, horses, cannons, armoured vans, commander-in-chief, heroes,

Rajput, invader, foreigner—from amongst them, I carefully picked and kept them under my wrap.

'Mr Askari, I want to lead a life with my wife and children. I could not, till now, free myself from customs and traditions. When I reach home with these words, you can't imagine the state of happiness in my family.'

I noticed a ray of hope in Askari's eyes. A smile danced on his lips. It seemed that the thought of creating a web out of the old words had instilled a new vigour. (Whereas I did not know how to create a world or web with words.) I spontaneously asked him: 'Why don't you contact poets and short story writers to sell your words?'

'Ah! They are the biggest source of words.'

Happily laden with words, I reached home. The darkness of the evening had spread all over. A dim bulb was lighted in the verandah. My wife, Sakina, was hovering like a shadow. My son, Imam, was probably sitting in the club. It was still not the time for his return.

'Sakina!' I called, and she swam to come out of the darkness. 'See, what I have brought?'

I spread out the old words on the nearby bed. Sakina's eyes bewilderingly stared at them. The reaction was visible on her face. She collected the words and looked for a safe place for their storage. I had not expected this reaction from her.

'What's the matter, Sakina? You should feel happy. They are treasures. With their help, we can arrive at the truth. And you...?'

'No!' Sakina waved away my proposal. 'This is not the right time. First, let me deal with them. Keep them away from the bookcase that is full of books. They may enter the pages of books and acquire their original positions.'

She removed the cluster from the bed. She carefully picked up the words and tied them to a bed sheet. Not a glimpse of the words was visible.

She came and sat by my side.

'What made you bring them home? You know a fire is raging outside.'

I saw hot liquid erupting on the deserted town far away in the background. The fires at night were scattering light on the town. Men, women, children, and even older people were running all over the place.

'Water,' they shouted but, instead, bottled fires were thrown at them. Vehicles stuffed with relief materials and currency notes screeched on the streets. But the fire raged. Some warmed themselves with the heat; others got burnt.

'You cannot prove words wrong till they become worn out and old,' I told Sakina. 'That is why I refused to take the new ones. Instead, I picked up old words with care. We will come to know the truth when we join all the words. Imam will also come to know about it. We have seen the books included in his syllabus. Are they dependable?'

'Don't start a discussion now.' There was a quiver in her voice. 'Imam is yet to get his board certificate. He still has to read what is written in his books. In the end, he has to choose between the earlier governments and present rulers.'

'Otherwise?' I asked.

'Choosing between right and wrong, Imam may not become the kind of hero whose morning begins in a Dubai hotel and night with girls of glitz and glamour. Who knows where youths in search of wealth may land up? Probably printing fake currencies?'

I thought Sakina was a mother. 'What about that suicide bomber?'

'Can the pursuit of lust ever be transferred into the love for the country? Have you ever seen a suicide bomber amidst those robbers who freely distribute food items? Yes, you must have seen people give up their uniforms and get court marshalled.' Her voice was normal.

I failed to understand her words.

'You are a mother.' I whispered in her ears. 'I do not know how many mothers have succeeded in keeping their sons in fetters.'

I drew her to myself.

Then one day, there was a devastating explosion. Sakina was burnt to ashes. My body was in splinters. The roof of the house blew up to the sky. The walls crumbled down to the ground. Smoke and darkness covered the place. Slowly the haze cleared. The surroundings became clearer and I saw it.

The circle of sparkling words was building a web high up in the air. But the collection of new words had completely succeeded in encircling the web; words that I had left behind at the shop.

'Oil, missiles, superpower, tanks—frenzy, courage, suicide bomber...'

SIMILAR

ANISUN NABI

Getting up from sleep, the seven young men felt fresh. One of them asked: 'How long did you sleep?'

The second replied: 'Either the whole day or less. God only knows how long we slept. We had never experienced such deep sleep.'

'That's right. We are feeling so refreshed.'

The third added: 'The cruel King Dakhyanus, wanted to kill us. We got saved from his clutches somehow. Had he managed to catch us, he would have stoned us to death. Or, forced us to be a part of his gang.'

'It seems God has placed a cover on the King's heart.' The fourth added with resentment. 'That stops him from being just. It has blocked his ears; making him incapable of hearing voices of justice and instruction.'

'Allah directed us to this huge Arrajeem cave,' Belal said with a sense of calm. 'We got saved.'

'The danger is not over yet,' Bin Yameen tried to shake off his companion's complacency. 'The King's army may arrive any time, looking for us. It's better to move out.'

'Not at all. This is a safe place,' Malikha stopped him short. 'The vast cave does not allow even the rays of the sun to enter. The mouth of the cave faces north. Irrespective of the seasons, the sun's rays do not penetrate. A passer-by won't know who is inside. We can safely reside here. Not that we are cowards,' he added after a thought. 'Neither are we scared of death nor do we love life. But we want to live. Before achieving the goal, we do not want to die.'

'But if we stay without food and water, far from reaching our objective, we will die. Our bodies would decay and decompose in this cave without even getting a decent burial.'

Malikha stared at the youth whose pangs of hunger made him add:

'Last night, we ran frantically for miles on an empty stomach. When endurance failed and food was not available, we collapsed at this spot.'

'Lover of food,' Malikha retorted with friendly banter. 'Think about ones languishing in prisons of Dakhyanus, without food and water, tortured physically, but not losing self-control.'

The words made the youth remember his friends. He became reflective.

To lighten his mood, Malikha tapped on his head and dangled a silver coin before his eyes. 'I'm going to bring bread for you. Meanwhile, control your hunger.'

Their conversation brightened up other faces, like the moon emerging out of dense clouds.

Keeping in mind the cheerfulness of his companions, Malikha emerged out of the cave.

The dog, at the mouth of the cave, started wagging its tail as soon as he saw Malikha. The faithfulness of the dog surprised him.

'You are still here! Now run away. If the Romans catch you, your faithful nature will come to an end.'

The dog started barking, making the others come out in the open. They stared at it in surprise.

'Isn't it the same dog that followed us amidst the sandstorm in the desert?'

'Yes. It was ahead of us; guided and lead us to this place.'

'God is Almighty and can make anyone perform the work of *Khizir*. Don't drive him away. He may also be hungry. I am going to town to fetch some bread.'

Malikha went down the hills and reached the town. He stood near a bakery. He sensed curious eyes staring at him. Hungry and tired, he looked around. A host of strange questions perplexed his mind.

'How can the world change in such a short time and space? Everything has changed overnight,' he ruminated. 'Men's faces, heights, style of living, culture and customs. How can they all undergo such a drastic change? God! Are these women?

They have no shame. How can the population explode all of a sudden? What has diminished the height of men? How can there be houses reaching almost the skies, skyscrapers? It seems every house contains a town within itself. Camels, horses, and donkeys have disappeared from the marketplace. How do people carry out their day-to-day activities without these animals?'

The horn from a car close by shook him up. He looked around, and his surprise knew no bounds. 'What magical entity is this?' he now questioned himself. 'How peacefully are men sitting inside it? The glitter and the glitz of passengers!' he wondered. 'It is better to stay away from the mysterious surroundings. Let me buy bread. Return to the cave. I have to feed hungry friends. They may be waiting.'

He stood before the baker.

Looking at his height, built, and dress, the baker looked bewildered. 'Who are you?' the baker asked in surprise.

Malikha didn't say much. He wanted to keep his identity under wraps.

But the baker was not satisfied with a few words. His curiosity about such a unique individual kept on increasing.

'Tell me, who are you?'

'I am a man,' Malikha quickly added.

'That I know. Where are you coming from?'

'Does that matter?' he replied. 'What if you come to know about me?'

'Nothing. I get bored,' the baker changed tact. 'By talking to customers, I develop intimacy. If you don't want to talk, it's okay. The cut and design of your dress seem natural,' the baker went on. 'There must be some fancy-dress competition in which you are participating.'

'I have no interest in what you say,' Malikha tried to look irritated in order to avoid such talks. 'Take the coin and give me bread.'

When the shopkeeper looked at the coin, his curiosity knew no bounds. He turned the silver coin upside down. 'Where did you get this coin?'

'What kind of a question is this?' Malikha got annoyed. 'You wasting time, talking nonsense.'

'It is not nonsense,' the shopkeeper surveyed the man with curious eyes and mumbled words to himself:

'This tall, sturdy, wheatish-complexioned man must have laid hands on some treasure.' Taking his doubt to be true, he hollered for men standing close by: 'Brothers, come and ask this weird man from where did he bring this centuries-old coin?'

'Mad man!' said Malikha, 'Do I look strange to you? You are a strange man. Don't you handle coins? Do you think this is a centuries-old coin? You are playing with fire.'

Taking the baker's words to be fit for nothing, Malikha tried to express his stand to the crowd that had gathered out of nowhere. But instead of taking him seriously, they started laughing.

'Why are you laughing at me?' Malikha's voice turned serious. 'I hate frivolity. I appreciate a standard of excellence. Do you understand?'

Failing to stop their mirth that hurt his feelings, he spoke in disgust: 'Oh Merciful and Generous! Where have you sent me? These are strange people. Instead of helping a traveller, they are harassing him. Who are these people?'

'They are Isaac, Tony, Webhishan, Mukrib, and Joseph.'

'They all stay here,' the baker said, hiding his sarcastic smile. 'Tell us, where are you from? Or forget it. Tell us, from where did you bring this centuries-old coin? Tell us, otherwise...'

'Otherwise what?' Malikha asked in anger. 'Will you hand me over to Dakhyanus? Do so.' He was losing his patience. 'The prison offered by Dakhyanus is better than a life of insult.'

'Who is Dakhyanus?' What are you talking about? I do not know any Dakhyanus?'

'You do not know Dakhyanus?' Malikha spoke in astonishment. 'Close by resides this dictatorial ruler. His cruelty, oppression and tyrannous rule made him infamous. And you are trying to feign ignorance? I understand your intention. You are part of his gang. Proving my coin outdated, you are showing moral degradation.'

'What moral degradation?' the baker lifted his voice. 'This coin is ancient. It belongs to very old times. It is a silver coin. Coins minted in silver belonged to olden times.'

'Man! Are you in your senses?'

'This trader remains in his senses. You are out of your mind. You refuse to listen to reason. It is better you do something about the aberration of your mind. For even a beggar here nowadays accepts a dollar rather than a coin. You are misleading a man of the world like me with this centuries-old coin! Unless you give me a dollar, I am not giving you bread.'

A fairly large crowd collected after hearing the heated conversation between Malikha and the baker.

A middle-aged, decent-looking man wriggled through the crowd, stood before them and spoke to the baker with seriousness.

'Show me the coin,' he said. 'I am a numismatist. I am an expert who knows everything about coins. I will be able to solve your problem with my knowledge.'

The man took over the coin from the baker and addressed Malikha: 'Don't be worried. In a strange place, I am your friend.'

For Malikha, the sudden help was like arriving at a date palm tree in the scorching afternoon desert.

The baker and the crowd waited patiently for the announcement from the numismatist. That would expose the reality of the stranger and his coin. After examining it with the criterion of his knowledge, he addressed Malikha, caught amidst the crowd, in a tone of mixed reaction.

'The coin,' the man chose his words with care, 'seems to be of ancient times. Probably centuries old. But the passage of time has failed to leave its imprint. It does not seem to have been buried below the earth. It seems to be strange. The coin contains the portrait of Emperor Decius. History tells us that he was the founder of the Roman Empire. I also know that the rule of Dakhyanus was marked by cruelty and tyranny. History is replete with stories of his brutality. But I fail to understand that by repeatedly taking the name of Dakhyanus, why are you making yourself a part of ancient history?'

'You are talking in their language,' Malikha said. 'I thought you were knowledgeable,' he went on with a sullen look. 'I was under the impression that you will give me my due.'

'That is what I am doing!'

'Then why are you denying my existence? Why are you trying to prove a man of flesh and blood, a centuries-old mysterious creature? The coin which fetched commodities 24 hours ago is being proved antique. For what sin are you punishing me?'

The numismatist, understanding the delicacy of the situation, quietly left the place.

The baker spoke to Malikha with restraint: 'Look. Tell me, who are you? Where are you coming from? From which society? A man of your height and stature cannot be found in today's world. Just think. We are not your enemy. We are awestruck at your weirdness.'

'I am surprised at yours,' Malikha said. 'I am surprised at your society, the times. I cannot understand how drastic changes have taken place. I wonder if the Creator again might not have uttered "*Kun*" to transform the world. Anyway, I can understand things. You are amongst those who sing paeans to hoarders and make others do whatever they want. I am not amongst those who give away self-respect for filling his stomach.'

The crowd watched him without batting an eyelid. One close by tried to buy bread and hand it over to him. Malikha reacted angrily: 'Why should I take bread from you? You refused the currency in vogue, proving it outdated. You hurt my dignity by proving the truth as false. I will return to tell six friends of mine that if Dakhyanus can place spies upon us, you people are playing with our hunger. Today the manner in which you have placed guards over the food; tomorrow, your progeny will restrict water. But remember, like Shaddad's Paradise, Qarun's wealth, and Pharoah's arrogance, Dakhyanus' cruel reign will also come to an end. The mercy of our Guide, that the great Heaven has bestowed upon him, will remain.'

Malikha left the place. On the baker's instruction, one of his servants followed him.

Malikha arrived at the cave. A young man, unable to bear the pangs of hunger, comes running: 'Now pangs of hunger will be there no more. Quickly give me bread.'

'Forget bread. I was insulted, disgraced. Managed to return alive.'

They look at Malikha's distraught condition in awe and shock.

'Don't you ask me what I have seen,' said Malikha. 'It was a waking dream. There was only one Dakhyanus. Here all of them have acquired his attributes. It was like being hanged in broad daylight. We have to leave immediately. It is possible someone might have followed me.'

The others pester for information from Malikha. After coming to know the facts, they get ready to leave the place when one of them, staring at the sky, looks perplexed.

'What kind of calamity is this? Nobody has seen anything like this before? Why is this airborne giant-eagle-like catastrophe hovering around our heads?'

'Be quiet,' Malikha whispered. 'Something like this had left me stunned. Let's us hide behind rocks and try to understand this weird thing.'

Bin Yameen's surprise knew no bounds. 'This weird thing must be a bird or else how could it flap its wings.'

'Look carefully,' the fourth added. 'It's something else, for this magical entity has within it a white man sitting inside. Till it goes away, we should wait.'

When calm was restored, they looked at each other with reassuring eyes.

'The danger is over. We can move.'

From the heights of the hills down to the plains, they searched for a place of refuge. Down the hill, they spotted a tent. They trudged down the tortuous paths. Malikha cautioned them: 'You have to save yourself from the calamity in the sky and the earth till you fulfil your objective. Below, there are the armies of Dakhyanus and the terror from the sky is in the form of the bird-like entity. The tent can provide us with a temporary shelter. All of you stay here while Bin Yameen and I do a survey.'

'You stay with them,' Bin Yameen replied. 'You have come out from one crisis. I don't want to lose you in a trifling endeavour. I will go with Bilal. If things are safe, I will ask everyone to come down. Otherwise, we will meet on the Day of Judgement.'

Both Bin Yameen and Bilal went down towards the tent. The youths prayed silently for them.

They were close to reaching the tent when the clattering sound from the sky rose once again in the air. They lifted up their eyes to find the airborne entity following them. They quickly increased their pace and ran. They managed to reach the tent and called the inmates. Some men came out of the tent and ushered them inside. They heaved a sigh of relief. It was like finding a patch of cloud on the vast spread-out desert. The sudden feeling of security made them swoon.

When they returned to their senses, they found themselves bound in chains. All over stood white men in uniforms, their faces betraying malicious smiles. The men were staring at their gigantic stature and built.

But on the faces of the two youths were many questions.

'Who are these people? Why have they chained us? What do they want from us? In what part of the country have we stepped in? We had run away from the terror of Dakhyanus. How come that in place of the old, our enemy now has become these white men? How strange is it? Will the terror and animosity of these strange enemies never come to an end?'

Bin Yameen courageously lifted his hands for prayer when a strange cry emitted out of his mouth: 'Look there! Another one is trying to make a landing near the cave. Oh God! What sound is this? Is it the end of the world?' Belal's curiosity increased: 'Look! The white creatures inside the eerie bird seem to be throwing something. The hills seem to vanish like specks of clouds. Why are they venting their anger on the stony cave?'

'This is just the beginning,' the white officer said, holding Belal by his hair. 'If you do not give answers to our questions, the outcome will be serious. In which rat hole is your leader hiding?'

'He is our guide and leader, not a rat that he would be hiding in a hole. We are peace-loving people. We are declaring our noble intentions before the public and Dakhyanus...'

'Enough of your Dakhyanus drama,' the officer said, holding a cane in his hand. 'The men at the marketplace have told us about your craftiness. Your dress, appearance and language cannot hide the reality. Try to understand.'

The officer changed his tone, thinking it may help him extract some information.

'If you tell us about the whereabouts of your leader, our government would give you so much money that you cannot imagine in your wildest of dreams. Besides that, beautiful girls, too, that in your holy book are referred to as virgins of heaven. In short, the gifts of the world would be at your feet. But if you do not, we will not hesitate to kill. So, you better tell us about your terrorist leader and his place of hiding.'

'Our guide is not a terrorist. He talks about peace and worldly brotherhood. He goes to the extent of saying that if someone smacks you on one face, advance the other before him. But on no occasion, take revenge. How can such a person become a terrorist? It is your cruel Dakhyanus who is, in fact, a terrorist. You are hand in glove with him. If you want to meet my guide and leader, then find him in the small cottage behind the palace of Dakhyanus. That is his place of residence. Go there and arrest him. He is not scared of the rigours of imprisonment; even death cannot force him to change his way of life.'

'What is he saying, sir?' a soldier, unable to understand Bin Yameen, asks his superior in a frustrated way.

The officer stares with hateful eyes and uses foul language.

'I know that physically you are strong. Even death will not be able to make you spill the secret. But I am not amongst those who will forgive the wrongs that have been committed by your leader, I mean your guide, as you wish to call him.'

'Are you in your senses?' Belal retorted with surprising courage. 'What wrongs are you talking about? What damage have we few peace-loving, unarmed people committed? Our guide has shown us the way to truth. He brought us from darkness to light, from idolatry, misconception, and false notions to the precincts of faith. From battles, hatred against nations and race, we have started a jihad against the desires, the self...'

'Right!' said the officer. 'That is the word: Jihad. Your leader has managed to influence idiots like you, brainwashed unformed young minds. You have brought down our international skyscrapers and tallest buildings that housed arms and ammunitions like houses of cards. We could not do anything to stop you.'

The officer's anger reached its peak. With bloodshot eyes, he beat the two with his belt till the skin peeled off.

Both of them were surprised at the sudden turn of events and prepared themselves for the worst.

The officer went close to them and said: 'So you will not divulge the dwelling of your leader?'

'The dwelling of the leader that you are talking about,' said one of the youths, 'is not known to us. You do not have faith in our guide. Now you have to decide.'

'The decision has been made,' the officer directed another.

The second soldier advanced with a knife.

Belal and Bin Yameen embraced each other for the last time.

The officer spoke, trying to hide his sense of defeat. 'When a thing or man is of no use, we destroy them. Prepare to die.'

'Death comes to the body,' Bin Yameen said, looking into the eyes of the white officer. 'Not to the soul. We two will die. But five are still living...'

THE WATCH

REYAZ DANISH

'Have you seen my watch?' Raj asked in his stentorian voice.

He had just returned from office and opened the cuff link of his right hand when his eyes fell on his wrist. His heart gave in. He looked into the wardrobe drawer where, apart from other items, he also kept his watch. When he failed to find it, he raised his voice to ask Sarita: 'Have you seen my watch?'

Sarita, who was kneading flour in the kitchen, came running into the room. Her right hand was smeared with flour.

'Why are you screaming?' she said weakly. The day's chores had brought fatigue to her voice.

Raj stared at his wife.

The ordinary cotton sari and her appearance could make one understand that somewhere in her lay hidden the pain of being the daughter-in-law in a middle-class family.

'I cannot find my watch,' he said.

'What do you mean?' asked Sarita in astonishment.

'That's it. I cannot find it.'

'You have returned from office. It should have been on your wrist.'

'Can't you see it is not?' He pointed to his wrist.

'You didn't take it off?'

'No!'

'Didn't you put it on when you left for office?'

'I can't remember.'

He tried to think hard, his eyes widening.

'If you didn't, then it must be here,' Sarita moved towards the wardrobe.

'No use. I have already searched in it.'

'Then it must be out here,' Sarita moved towards the dressing table. 'You have a habit of keeping it here too.'

Some dirty linen was strewn over the dressing table. When Sarita picked them up, she found Soni's teddy bear tucked inside. She kept the bear in place and muttered: 'Both father and daughter have the habit of scattering things and forgetting.'

Then she addressed her daughter, who was studying, perched on a chair beside her study table. 'Soni! Take care of your teddy. No one will do it for you... What makes you stare?' She spoke to the husband. 'Go and change! I'll wash my hands and be back soon.'

She went into the kitchen and returned with a glass of water.

Raj changed and went into the bathroom to freshen himself. His clothes were casually thrown on the bed. After keeping the glass on the dressing table, she gathered the clothes, and put them on the hanger. She placed the hangers inside the wardrobe and tidied the bed. She looked around to see if she could find the missing watch.

Raj sat and thought but failed to remember whether he had worn it or not while leaving for office. He again put the same question to his wife.

'Did you find it?'

She nodded her head.

'How can it vanish?' he spoke to himself.

'Can't you recollect whether you had worn it while leaving for office?'

'I told you I don't remember.'

'Tell me,' Sarita said, trying to help him. 'Did you see the time on your watch at the office?'

'When do I find time for it?' he said. 'If I need, I look at the office clock.'

While looking around the room, Sarita spotted Soni. The girl had placed her elbows on the rim of the table and, with her head on her folded palms, was watching her mother. The pencil was stuck between her fingers.

'Soni!' Sarita said. 'Have you seen Papa's watch?'

'No.'

'Now don't just stare,' Sarita admonished her. 'Focus on your studies.'

'Okay, Mummy,' the girl said.

'Could it have fallen off?' a sudden idea flashed in Raj's mind as he gulped down the water.

'Fall off?' Sarita said as if lightning had struck her. 'But where could it fall?'

'Anywhere … in the bus … at the office …'

'Bus … office,' Sarita repeated the words as if she could not come out of the shock.

'Yes. It could have fallen off anywhere. Now it is gone. I won't get it back. For some time, I had noticed that the chain had become loose. I couldn't have imagined it would come off. How careless of me. I wasn't even conscious when it dropped.'

'Tomorrow enquire at the office,' she tried to help him again. 'God willing, you may get it back. It was a token of remembrance of my father.'

'If someone had picked it up at the office,' he replied. 'Do you think he will return it?'

'If he's a virtuous soul, he will.'

'Just a minute,' he interrupted her. 'From office, I had been to Ramesh's house. It is possible I might have dropped it there.'

'Did you go to Ramesh Bhai's place?'

'Yes. He always complains that I have changed after marriage. I don't visit him nowadays. So today, I wanted to clear up his misgivings.'

'Everyone is fine at his place?' She asked casually.

'Yes.'

'Good, you paid them a visit. He also stopped calling us for quite some time. He must have become displeased.'

'Hmm. I don't even ring him nowadays.'

'Why don't you do so now?' her eyes brightened up. 'Also, enquire about the watch.'

When Raj dialled him, there was no dial tone on the telephone. He angrily put the receiver back in its place. 'It's dead.'

'What! The phone is dead! That's why no one called the whole day.'

Raj collapsed on the sofa.

'Don't waste time,' Sarita said. 'Go to the PCO and call him.'

'Forget it,' Raj said. 'Suppose it has fallen in Ramesh's house; I will get it back.' He soon looked around and said: 'Where is Babuji?'

'Where else can be he? Must be with his friends … Playing cards … Would you like a cup of tea?'

'Oh! Yes.'

Sarita went into the kitchen.

When Raj followed her there, she asked him: 'Have you succeeded in recollecting ...'

'No,' Raj said, taking out a bottle from the fridge. 'Can't recollect anything. I do remember taking it out of the wardrobe. Now whether I had left it on the dressing table or not!' Then he thoughtfully said, 'Can anyone have entered my room after I left for office? I mean someone from the neighbourhood?'

'Some children were there,' Sarita said. 'They played with Soni in the drawing room and then left. I was with them. I didn't see anyone enter your room.'

'Are you sure?'

'Of course. After you left, only Babuji went inside. That too, to get the newspaper.'

Nobody knows what insinuation the thought contained that both furtively stared at each other. Their eyes met. The unexpressed thought that language failed to communicate was articulated, even understood, without words. Both averted their eyes. The call bell rang. Raj went and opened the door.

Babuji, in a white dhoti and kurta, stood smiling in his characteristic way. But the worry on the face of his son made his smile vanish.

'What makes you worried?' he asked.

'It's nothing,' Raj tried to look normal.

'You can't hide it from your father.' He called the daughter-in-law, who came running.

'Why is he worried?' Babuji asked. 'Have I died?'

'God Forbid!' Sarita said. 'Wash yourself. I will make tea for both.'

Sarita avoided answering his question and went into the kitchen.

'He is not saying anything,' Babuji said. 'She is refusing to reply. There is something wrong. Soni! Where are you?'

'Yes, Dadaji,' Soni ran towards him.

'Have they quarrelled, your mummy and papa?' the old man asked.

'No,' said Soni.

'Then what is the matter?' He again asked the girl.

'Papa cannot find his watch,' Soni simply said.

Babuji stared at Raj, who was sitting on the sofa.

'Which one? That which you used to wear?' he asked Raj.

'Yes.'

'That your father-in-law gave at the time of your marriage?'

'Yes.'

'How much could have been its cost?'

'Around 2,000.'

'Now it cannot even be 500.'

'It was Japanese,' Raj said with annoyance. 'Japani ...'

'Once it was. Now it's only "*pani*", useless.'

'During these seven years, it never went out of order,' Raj added.

'So what! It was old after all.'

'It was a token of remembrance of Sarita's father. Close to my heart. God knows where I dropped it.'

'Was it in working condition?'

'Sure!'

'Must have gone out for some work.'

'Babuji, my watch has been stolen. I mean lost. You are making fun of it. Just think how bad Sarita would have felt about it.'

'I know. What can be done about it? Buy a new one.'

'Can such a watch be found? Do I have money to buy one?'

'Now something which you cannot afford to buy, or which had become rare, should have been handled with care. You do not even know whether it has been stolen or lost? Will anyone leave such a watch if he finds it? An unemployed man like me will certainly not. Now forget lamenting about the watch. Tell *bahu* to send my cup of tea to my room.

***

It was one o'clock at night. Raj lay on the bed. Sarita was on the other side. They were breathing and still awake. The thoughts of the watch were still on their minds.

'Where… where!' It brought up enormous possibilities. The mental turmoil made them seek answers in farfetched areas.

Sarita turned around and stared at Raj.

'Still awake?'

'Yes, you too?'

'I cannot sleep.'

'Sarita,' Raj spoke softly. 'I have made a blunder.'

'Blunder? How?'

'I never gave pocket money to Babuji. Never asked him about his needs. Took for granted that he does not need money. A retired man also has needs; it diminishes but does not end.'

Raj said it but could not believe what his own ears heard. The open admission was an encouragement of thoughts that were striking him like a poisonous snake. He had been trying his best to stop them.

'That's right. It is already six months of his retirement.'

Though Sarita's words were an admission of his mistake, he heard something break within, bruising him. The meaning he could infer from his wife's words was this: 'He had retired; his savings must have been exhausted.'

'I think,' Raj said, 'it is better to give him pocket money.'

'That's the right thing to do,' Sarita yawned. 'Now sleep. You have to get up in the morning.' She put her head on his lap. Soon her snores rang in the air. Raj tried his best to sleep but failed. He was having a tussle with something inside him. He was trying to place logic in order to come out of the dilemma.

It would have gone throughout the night had he not, like his wife, been enveloped by sleep in the later part of the night.

***

Raj was having his breakfast. He looked pale because of last night's sleeplessness. The scuffle of thoughts still raged within him. He didn't see when Babuji came and sat at the table. He shook himself when Babuji said: 'Did you find your watch?'

'Can it be found?' Raj said with hopelessness.

'Right,' said Babuji, 'So forget it. Enjoy your food.'

'I am trying,' Raj said.

'I see. Your face shows you had spent a sleepless night.'

Babuji knew something was wrong. Raj tried to change the topic.

'What are you going to do today?'

'What can a retired man do?' Babuji quickly said. 'In other words, you can say that a man of no work has enough of it. Why do you ask me?'

'The phone is dead. Can you go and file a complaint?'

'Okay. On my way to the pension office, I will do it.'

'Has your pension not been cleared yet?'

'The clerk is still withholding the file.'

'Why?'

'You being a clerk, should know it,' Babuji replied. 'Unless you give them a bribe, no file moves.'

'What will you do?'

Babuji stopped him in the midst and said: 'In the beginning, I tried to be a Gandhi follower. But then I thought that if I remained a Gandhi*waad*, then even my clothes would be taken away from me. Like Gandhi, I would only be seen in a dhoti. It is good that in our country, we have the custom of bribes. If not, then 90 per cent of the population would have been below the poverty line.'

'I don't agree,' Raj said. 'A man should lead an honest life.'

Though Raj used the words in general, the insinuation could not be missed.

'When did I say I wanted you to agree with me? If you want to spend life with honesty, then be it so. I have done away with it.'

'Have the principles you propounded all your life gone to tatters? Was this the lesson that you taught me?'

'Had I done so, I would have gone to the burning *ghat* without my pension,' Babuji said with earnestness on his face, which he quickly hid in his characteristic smile.

'I don't want to argue,' Raj said, giving in. His father smiled, and Raj went to his room. He soon came out with a 500 rupee note and gave it to his father.

Babuji cast a cursory glance at the note and asked: 'You want me to fetch something for you?'

'No. This is for your pocket expense.'

'Pocket expense? For me?' The same smile danced on Babuji's face. 'Do you think that without my pension, I am out of my mind? Have I lost my morality? So that I may retain my morality, you are giving me a bribe?'

'Neither do I believe in taking a bribe nor giving it. At least I will never do so to my father. Don't think I am such a worthless man.'

'When did I ever take you to be a worthy one,' Babuji said, leaving the breakfast table. '*Bahu*!' He lifted his voice. 'Bring two cups of tea to my room. Today is a day of enjoyment. A son has given pocket expense to his father.'

Babuji went into his room.

***

At six in the evening, the bell rang. Sarita opened the door. As expected, she found Raj standing there. By looking at his face, Sarita could understand that there must be good news.

'Got the watch?'

'How did you know?' Raj asked, entering the room.

'It was written on your face. Where did you get it?'

'At Ramesh's house.'

'You went there?'

'When there was no news at the office, I rang up Ramesh. I came to know that it had fallen near the sofa where I sat,' Raj said, handing over the watch to his wife. 'It had stopped. Now it has to be repaired.'

'Had you rang him yesterday, you would have been saved from the trouble.'

'That's right. Ramesh tried, but... is the phone now in order?'

'Yes. It is working.'

'Babuji must have filed the complaint. Where is he?'

'He left after breakfast. Has not returned. Didn't even come for lunch.'

Raj looked despondent. He was feeling a sense of guilt. Sarita also felt it deeply, and the atmosphere turned tense.

'Tomorrow, repair the watch,' Sarita said in order to make the situation light.

The doorbell rang. When Raj opened the door, he found his father with his characteristic smile.

Babuji sat on the sofa.

'Do you know the bribe worked wonders?' the old man said. 'My pension has started. I also got my gratuity. I have deposited the gratuity amount in the fixed deposit in my granddaughter's name. You people have no right over it. It can either be used for her higher education or marriage.'

Babuji thought for a while. He took out a watch from his pocket. He put it on Raj's palms and added: 'Here is your favourite watch. Doesn't it look like the earlier one?'

He then addressed his daughter-in-law: '*Bahu*, send me a cup of tea in my room.'

He then looked at his son: 'What makes you stare? Put it on your wrist. The shopkeeper had adjusted the time. If that other one was a token of remembrance of your father-in-law, this one is of your father's.'

Babuji went into his room.

There were two watches in Raj's hand, both identical. One showed the right time; the other didn't.

***

WHEN PEACE CAME AROUND

REYAZ DANISH

After the morning prayer, on the lawns of the *khanqah*, the *qawwal*s had set their stage; the song, accompanied by music, began: 'The morning breeze had intimated the news/ knowing the self bestows kingship… bestows kingship… kingship...'

The *qawwal*s sang and sunshine gradually spread over the vicinity of the building. Life languorously came out of its slumber. People carried on with daily chores. Everything went on so quietly that one was not even conscious of them. But something unusual happened at the corner of the *khanqah*. Sheikh Sahab was absent at the morning prayer. Was he ill? Taking rest in the inner room?

That was far from it.

Today, he was in deep anguish. He could not sleep. He prayed the whole night and expressed forgiveness. But the night was agonising; the worst in a century. Though he tried to develop contact with God, like a stray calf, he went on mooing in the dark jungle. The night for him did not end with the dawn. Like an adder, it squatted inside him. Tired of facing the snake, he would come out and stroll. The songs of the *qawwals* were irritating, making him impatient. His body trembled; the *qawwal*s went on with their songs, in ecstatic disposition, accompanied with music: 'The morning breeze had intimated the news ...'

After sunshine spread over the vicinity, Sheikh Sahab knew it was unbecoming of him to stay pent up. He came out. Life moved in its usual way. He crossed the verandah to arrive at the locale of the tomb. Accidentally, his eyes fell on the tomb's window screens. Thousands of threads had been tied by devotees. His eyes spotted hands that quivered to tie the devoted threads, souls whose only hope was pinned on those tender threads. They were those who had pawned their peace with the tying of threads. Will they get their peace? Has anybody got it? Will anybody ever get it? The only thought that was moving in his mind was: Peace was nowhere... It's just nowhere...

Lost in his thoughts, Sheikh Sahab crossed the vicinity of the shrine to climb onto the steps wrenched out of the hilly terrains. He reached the point from where the aerial view of the shrine could be seen. Whenever impatient, he came here to calm his ruffled soul. But today, he failed to calm the storm within. He closed his eyes. He wanted his mind to come out of it. He could hear the faint voices of the *qawwal*s: 'Your life is with it … your respect too … if character upheld… kingship… if effaced…disrepute…'

Sheikh Sahab had hardly spent a few moments of solitude when a voice startled him.

'Sorry for the interruption, Sheikh Sahab! Had my last night's question crossed the boundaries of decency?'

Sheikh Sahab recognised the voice immediately. He was the devotee who had followed him up the steps of the hillock.

He turned around to find the man with a questioning look behind him.

This man arrived here months ago and had become his devotee. He had come with sadness in his eyes. His irregular manner was a sign of some mishap. His ruffled hair, an insight into his convoluted life; his dry lips an indication of unquenched thirst. He was distraught and in quest of peace. One day moving around the shrine, Sheikh Sahab had spotted the man. He was crying inconsolably, holding the tomb's window screen. The Sheikh was touched. He took the man into the inner chamber. He consoled and invited him to stay at the *khanqah*.

After accepting the initiation, the man left no stone unturned to serve his master; he made religious practice the mission of his life. Slowly his life developed an order, his mannerism a symmetry. His ruffled hair did not look dishevelled; his dry lips came back to life. But the sadness in his eyes was replaced with impatience. He apparently looked peaceful but, in reality, was not, like a river that looks tranquil on the top and restless within. The search for peace that brought him here was yet to be found. His search went on; impatience not over, sadness still a part of his self.

That is why Sheikh Sahab addressed his followers last night, saying:

'Committing of sin is not against man's nature. What is alien is his not repenting. When you cross the limits of human nature, repent for your act. Seek forgiveness. Examine your conduct in the light of your conscience. You will come to know that from the state of man, you have risen to that of an angel! Remember, man is an embodiment of flaws. Only God … so devotees … If God has made us full of flaws, He has bestowed upon us the power of reason. It guides us to the right path. Whenever the seeds of sin begin to grow, hold the stick of reason. When the ups and downs of life weaken you, use the power of reason. You will see the right path. Peace will be your companion….'

Sheikh Sahab had hardly reached the point when the interruption took place.

'I beg permission,' someone said with reverence.

It caused a stir. The devotees stared in disbelief. Sheikh Sahab was taken aback but controlled himself and said: 'You are permitted.'

'Your respected self said that one can get peace by walking the paths of reason. In my case, it is reason that is creating problems. If it provides answers, it gives rise to new questions.'

'What is your problem?' Sheikh Sahab closed his eyes as if that would help him enter the region of thought, heart, and surroundings.

'My problem is my reason, guilt, peace; unbridled horses that bring me to a point where other paths branch out without real way: paths from which I had taken flight. I become frustrated. I find devotion and prayers futile. I prefer death to life.'

The last words made the Sheikh stare in disbelief. He cast a cursory glance at the devotees around. The stony-faced men were all ears, listening to interactions, babbling amongst themselves. Sheikh Sahab, with a wave of his hands, made them quiet. He looked at the man and said:

'When man becomes distressed, his mind agonised, he prefers death. Sin must have made way to his self. Sin that is yet to be resolved fails to lift him from the state of man to that of the angel.'

'If repentance of sin makes one an angel,' the devotee said, 'when can one become a man in the real sense? For to me, becoming a man is more difficult than becoming an angel.'

'You mean?' Sheikh Sahab asked in astonishment.

'I mean…,' the man left it midway, unsaid.

He could visualise his city torn asunder because of unrest. He saw lanes and houses where barbarity was at its peak.... People were killing each other, dying, houses burnt, hutments aflame, women raped, virginity lost.... He visualised swords held high up in the air. He saw a child's head on a sword and heard the heart-rendering shriek of a mother. Then silence ...

In the midst of the hushed calm, the devotee, breaking free of his thoughts, arranging his thoughts, wrenching free from the world of contemplation, then managed to say:

'I mean to ask: What is the repentance after killing a child?... Is repentance enough? Can words provide everlasting peace to the grieving mother? Can prayer protect the murderer from the curse of the mother? Or can it make the murderer say he had not committed the crime?'

The atmosphere turned gloomy. Men sat as if they were not of flesh and blood.

Sheikh Sahab looked at him and opened his mouth. Though his voice spread, it seemed a part of the silence that had pervaded the place.

'No good deeds can undo the murder of a child,' the Sheikh felt his voice quiver. He stressed upon words, chewing them. 'No language can express the pains of a mother...'

He felt as if chewing the words was bruising them; stressing was making the words lose their sense. He felt it better to remain quiet. But he went on, which made him feel helpless. 'No sentence can provide perpetual peace to the mother. And, as far as my knowledge is concerned, no prayer can save the murderer from the mother's curse. No practice can make the murderer believe he had not committed the murder. But in all this, what is important is the acceptance that the crime had been committed.'

At this point, Sheikh Sahab tactfully tried to control his voice; he, who had opted for silence, now thought it prudent to continue. 'Sin is manifest in everyone. But few have the feeling of guilt. This is what turns a human into a man. This is what shows us the way to become a better and successful man. This is what stops us from committing sin further. It is expiation from sin; of crimes that knowingly or unknowingly, are committed by us.'

'When does this sense of guilt appear in us?'

'When our reason mounts the stallion of guilt.'

'If acceptance of sins helps us become a better man, then what is the use of prayers?' The man asked with innocence.

'Herein we find peace... eternal peace.'

With the word 'peace', the silence in the room became intense, as if everything had reached a kind of satisfaction except the devotee himself. A sense of dissatisfaction failed to move him. The Sheikh was fully aware of it. So, he addressed him:

'Do you still have questions that may be striking like an adder?'

'If questions come to an end, then what would happen to answers? It is just like thinking about sin without grace, night without day, and death without life.'

'That's right. The flavour of life lies in contrasts. Makes us conscious of our existence, before the feeling of non-existence takes over our self. So whatever energises our self is this idea of contrast. Anyway, now ask your question.'

'I don't want to hurt anybody. I, therefore, have some hesitation.'

'Ask without hesitation. People come here in search of something. They go back satisfied. You, too, will not return unsatisfied. Your doubting mind will be content. Your search for the lost objective will come to an end.'

The Sheikh smilingly looked at the man, caught in a dilemma whether to express his desire or not.

It seemed the man had made up his mind.

'I do not know,' the man said, 'why you took up the life of a religious mendicant? Preferred asceticism in place of the glamour of life? But supposing, I say, only supposing, that you might have killed an innocent child. Or, as penitence for other crimes, taken up this mendicant way of life… May I ask that after years of devotion and prayer, have you made yourself free from the feeling of sin? Come out of its anguish? Have you derived peace in pursuit of which you changed the course of your life?'

The questions shook up the Sheikh. It was like an evil spirit had encircled him. It seemed his last drop of blood had been squeezed out, making him incapable of action or thought. He was reduced to dust. He was not conscious of the fleeting moments, silence, or how he left the place to enter his inner chamber.

Now, again, the man was standing before him like a question mark, seeking an answer. The Sheikh surveyed him from head to foot. If no satisfying answer emerged, then he would be hanging on the Cross of his question. The unnecessary spilling of the blood, so to say, would make the existence of the Sheikh hang on the Cross of his own conscience.

Both looked at each other with quiet eyes. The *qawwal*s went on with their songs: 'You didn't give me a hint of the destination … Oh, Wise man … /Why must I complain against you. You being neither the guide nor the traveller … the guide nor the traveller.… This, the message is being given…'

The Sheikh beckoned him and sat on a rock. He spoke in measured language.

'Your question didn't bother me,' the Sheikh began. 'An old wound burst open, which I thought had been healed. It was good. The apparently healed wound would have turned into an ulcer.'

'I fail to understand!' the man said.

'I know. I also know you are not satisfied here. You think all prayers, devotion, your own self, are a mere sham. But think, where do you not find pretence and deception? Man is inclined to deceive himself. When all roads seem blocked, the only way left is the *maa'rifat*, the faith in the Imam. Therein lies peace ...'

'Have you got peace?' the devotee's words unknowingly hurt him like a lancet.

The Sheikh's face at once changes various colours and they get mixed with one another.

'I wish I had...'

'Wish!' There was a surprise in the devotee's voice.

'Yes, I only wish I had... Stains of sins are never washed away. They pursue us.'

'Even you ...?'

'Yes, even me.' The Sheikh stopped in the midst of the songs that filled the air: 'The verse which is in the offing... The beggars know the rituals, of the other ... of the other ...'

'What makes you look so lost?'

'Lost? No. I have found my own self. This process of discovery is an awareness of one's self. It is a painful process. But nonetheless an honour.'

He looked at the Sheikh. The wise man stared far and beyond as if trying to catch hold of some long-lost moment.

Finally, he said: 'I do not know how you will assess me. Or, how God will treat me when I stand before him. But I know that my conscience has not freed me. This judge that spares none, may be why, even today, my ears still hear the words: "Baba".'

'Baba?' the devotee asked in surprise.

'Yes! That is how she would address me.'

'Who was she?'

'She was a young girl of 22 whose eyes had the innocent sparkle of a squirrel.'

Both the Sheikh and his devotee were silent. The sound of music filled the air; the song of the *qawwal*s rose intermittently: '... The knowledge of the self leads to Kingship.'

'It's about those days when...,' the Sheikh wandered into the past.

It's about the days when the Sheikh was around 45 or so. He was known in society as Farid Khan. He had his family business with ample turnover. He had a faithful wife and a daughter, 10 years old. He also ran a social organisation in his spare time, for nature had not only been bountiful, but he was also instilled with love for his fellow beings. With the help of this organisation, he tried to uplift the downtrodden, financially and psychologically, making them capable of leading respectable lives in society. Society, too, in return, looked upon him with respect. He had to undertake frequent trips relating to his business and the social organisation. It was on one of these trips that he met an innocent girl. The girl had run away with her lover, who turned out to be a fraud and tried to molest her. Farid Khan took pity on her and brought her home. His wife, who had a soft heart, agreed to give her shelter. Soon the girl became a part of the household. She became very friendly with Farid's daughter. She was educated and took the responsibility of teaching Farid Khan's daughter. Both the husband and wife tried their best to send her back home, but she declined. Farid Khan appointed her as a teacher in his social organisation, where her job was to educate the poor and underprivileged children. As a consequence of showing her gratitude, she addressed Farid Khan as 'Baba', who, in return, accepted her as his daughter. The boat of life moved on smoothly when suddenly it chanced upon an unexpected whirlpool. It was a hot afternoon. No one was present in the house. When Farid Khan entered, he found the girl asleep on the bed; her breast heaving up and down inside her *dupatta*. She was attractive; every part of her body was alive while she slept. Then the moment arrived that eliminated the relationship between the 'baba' and the 'daughter'. It was a lust-driven man and a woman lost in slumber. The man tried to steal the enchantment of sleep from the woman. The woman tried to make an attempt to save her virginity. But the dream was shattered when it dashed against the rock of reality; the man succeeded in running away with her siesta.

He left behind one who tried to gather her dashed dreams and a body neither dead nor with the capacity of life. After this, the girl retreated into her shell, shocked and lost. Farid Khan, too, became restless; his life on the edge. The sleep that he had unknowingly stolen now made him sit up at night. It turned into an agony when the girl, as usual, addressed him as 'Baba'. It seemed as if someone was abusing him. A word that once was a term of respect now became abusive. It was difficult to bear any longer. In the beginning, he was scared that the girl might go and break the news to the world. Now he wanted the girl to spit on him, call him names. He was ready to face ignominy but not hear the word 'Baba'. Even hundreds of lashes would appear like a balm on his skin. One day, finding it congenial, he asked her forgiveness for the mistake. He requested her not to use the word anymore. A smile appeared on the lifeless lips of the girl. It spoke about the pains of her life. Then her lips quivered and mournful words filled the air: 'Chastity is such that till it is not ravaged, becomes a load on the woman. I saved it from my lover who tried to rob me of it. If I had saved it from you, someone else would have ravaged it. The world never rests until it rips off the chastity of a lone woman. What's wrong if a dream is shattered, a delusion cleared? What's wrong with it? Someone just drank the whole water of the river to quench his thirst. Why bother if the river is now dry? When the river will overflow again, someone will come to quench his thirst. This is an age-old sport. You should not apologise for it. If there is no shame, why feel ashamed? Supposing I forgive, can you forgive yourself? Will the court of yourself release you? Now, as far as the usage of the word is concerned, I will go on using it. I have always seen you from that angle. Even today, I find the same fatherly affection in your eyes; and with it, the helplessness of a father whose daughter's chastity had been taken away!'

Farid Khan's court did not release him. One day he became a part of the dark night. Running away from the past memories, he found himself one morning in this *khanqah*.

There was peace on the Sheikh's visage when he finished his story. As if a burden had been lifted. But the restlessness of the devotee did not die down.

The devotee said: 'So after long years of prayers and devotion…'

'Yes! Even after years of devotion, if I happen to meet her and she addresses me as "Baba", I will feel abomination in my heart. It will renew the process of purification.'

The Sheikh saw a new sparkle in the eyes of his devotee. The Sheikh found him covering the rest of his journey in the arc of this newfound sparkle.

'Any more question?' the Sheikh asked.

'No. I have arrived at an answer.'

'What's that?'

'I have decided to leave this place.'

'Where to?' the Sheikh asks in astonishment.

'To that same sin-filled world without which we cannot understand the depth of our purgation. Atonement for sin is punishment. It is meaningless to stay here any longer.'

He wished the Sheikh '*Khuda Hafiz*' while the *qawwal*s went on with their song: 'The matter is delicate, if you agree then do/For you could not concur with the ways of the *khanqah*… this way of the *khanqah*… this way!'

GLOSSARY

The Dawn of Realisation

Didi: Elder sister

Jija: Brother-in-law

Swayamvar: In ancient India, a ceremony took place where unmarried ladies chose their grooms from a group of young men

Eyesore

Aanchal: The border or hem of the sari worn by women

Bhajan: Devotional songs

Ghat: Slope or flight of steps that leads to a river

Haveli: A huge mansion

Hukkah: Tobacco smoke drawn from a container fitted with pipe. An indispensable part of the 18th and 19th century aristocratic class. It became out of use but has now made a comeback in posh cafés and restaurants in metropolitan cities

Zamindar: A landlord

A New Tenant

Cuttacki masala-wala: Shopkeeper from Cuttack, Odisha, selling spices

Ghazal: A short poem popularised in Persian and Urdu. The 19th-century Urdu poets of India made it a household name. It is still popular because of its self-contained ideas within two lines

Mohalla: An area in a town or village, or collection of community houses in poorer parts of the city

Paan shop: Shop where betel leaves are sold

Rubaiyat of Khayyam: *Rubaiyat*, verse form of four-line stanzas made famous by Persian and Urdu poets. Khayyam refers to Omar Khayyam (1048–1131), the great Persian poet of the 12th century from Iran. He was also a mathematician, astronomer, and philosopher. He was made famous in the West by Fitzgerald's translation of his *rubaiyats* in English

Insight

Maidan: Open field

Shamiana: Tent or canopy erected during cultural/religious functions.

A Story Heard Before

Bhabi: Sister-in-law

The Inner Fort

Angarkhas and *Sherwanis*: Dresses worn by gentlemen of a particular class, now almost out of fashion

Ayaats: Verses of the Holy Quran

Benarasi: Here it refers to Benarasi sarees famous for their intricate and traditional designs worn especially during marriages

Bidi: Tendu leaf filled with tobacco, tied with a string and smoked as an alternative to cigarettes

Chun, Chun: Jingling sound

Darood: A type of prayer to praise and honour Prophet Muhammed (Peace be upon Him)

Ghagra choli: Dress worn by women in North India

Ghat: Slope or flight of steps that leads to a river

Haveli: A huge mansion

Huzoor: Term of respect

Laddoos, batashas: Sweets commonly eaten in India

Maghrib Azaan: The call for prayer during the evening

Maghrib: Evening prayer

Namaaz: The ritual prayers prescribed by Islam to be observed five times a day

Paan: Betel leaves

Qamarband; Ornaments worn by women around the waist

Salwar Kameez: Women's attire popular in all parts of India

Tehsil: An administrative area in parts of India

Tika: Forehead ornament worn by women during festive occasions

Tonga, Tum Tum, Ekka: Different kinds of carriages drawn by one or two horses

Tongawallah: Hackney carriage driver

The Stopped Clock

Banian: Vest or undergarment used in the subcontinent

Chops: A savoury

Cinder Patti: A particular area where ashes are stored

Khaini: Chewing tobacco used in the subcontinent

Samosas: Spicy potato-filled triangular shaped savoury, popular in the subcontinent

Agony

Bidi: Tendu leaf filled with tobacco, tied with a string and smoked as an alternative to cigarettes

Jhuggis: Dwellings in a slum made out of mud, tin, etc

Lungi: A garment similar to a sarong, wrapped around the waist and extending to the ankles, worn in in Southeast Asia

Plastic *motis*: Plastic beads

Sugarcane *Wallah*: A person selling sugarcane

The Wedding Register

Moulvi: A Muslim doctor of law or one who is learned in Islamic theology. But loosely, it refers to one who is religious and follows the tenets of Islam in everyday life

Nikah: Marriage contract in Islam between the bride and bridegroom at the time of marriage, solemnised by a *qazi*

Qazi: Usually a judge or one well versed in Shariat laws. He also performs other judicial functions like solemnising a Muslim marriage

A Half-Serious Story

Khuda Hafiz: Literally meaning: 'May God be your Protector'

Paan: Betel leaf

Psyche

Ayaat ul Kursi: Another verse from the Quran with mystical powers and is recited in prayers

Bhoot: Ghost

Dua: Invocation to God with open palms after every prayer

Ekka: Two-wheeled vehicle pulled by a horse. It is still popular in villages of India

Nullah: Ravine or a watercourse usually overflowing with dirty water

Surah-e Naas/Falaq/Ikhlas: All three Quranic verses are said to have powers to drive out evil forces

Surah-e-Fatiha: The verse at the beginning of the Holy Quran. It is mandatory to recite in every prayer and is said to contain mystical powers

Epic of the New Colony

Bustee: Slums or community houses in the poorer part of the city. Here the writer uses it in the sense of a colony

Karbala: A city in Iraq housing the shrine of Imam Hussain. The Prophet's grandson was killed in the battle of Karbala. Shias and Sunnis regard him as a martyr

*Lathi*s: Sticks

The Shop of Words

Salaam: Common salutation

Similar

Arrajeem cave: The cave where the men slept for years

Dakhyanus: Here it refers to the Roman Emperor Decius who ruled from AD 249–251. But it usually refers to one who is backward in thoughts

Khizir: In Islamic tradition, *Khizir* is a messenger who comes to the aid of people in need and possesses secret knowledge of the unseen. There are various stories where he is said to have met and helped even kings and rulers

Pharaoh: Egyptian kings who ruled for centuries. They were, over the period of time, referred to as Pharaohs. They were also believed to act as intermediaries between God and the people on earth

Qarun: He is also known as Croesus and lived probably during the time of Moses. Traditions speak of his immense wealth and grandeur and count him as one of the richest of men. His stories are still in vogue

Shaddad: He is said to be the King of the lost city of Arabia, which was destroyed by natural calamities. He is said to have built a heaven on earth but failed to enjoy it. The tales of the city's splendour are still spoken of and listened to with awe

The Watch

Bahu: Daughter-in-law

Gandhi*waad*: To follow the principles of Mahatma Gandhi

When Peace Came Around

Dupatta: A piece of cloth or scarf worn around the shoulders by women in the subcontinent

Khanqah: Monastery or building meant for spiritual retreat, rest and reformation. Also, a place for devotees, travellers and the public

Maa'rifat: Mystic knowledge

Qawwal: Professional singers of religious or Sufi songs accompanied by music. Later, they also sang popular songs and became part of marriage parties even in the early part of the 20th century

ACKNOWLEDGEMENTS

My grateful acknowledgements to the following copyright holders for permission to translate and reprint copyrighted material in this volume.

The stories 'Eyesore', 'A New Tenant', and 'The Dawn of Realisation' are taken from *Chehre Ki Wapsi*, published by Maktab-e-Talimaat, Kolkata, 1982. The stories are printed by the permission of Mahjabeen Sayeed, wife of Late Sayeed Premi, legal copyright owner.

The story 'Insight' is taken from *Naqsh Bar Aab*, published by Firoz Abid, Calcutta, 1984. The story 'Scenes Behind Scenes' is taken from *Andhi Gali Me Subah*, published by Firoz Abid, Calcutta, 1981. The stories are printed by the permission of the author.

The stories 'A Story Heard Before' and 'The Inner Fort' are taken from *Gadagar Sarai* by Anis Rafi, Modern Publishing House, New Delhi, 2016. The stories are printed by the permission of the author.

The stories 'The Stopped Clock', 'Agony', and 'The Wedding Register' are taken from *Mare Huye Aami Ki Laltain*, by Siddique Alam, Educational Publishing House, Delhi, 2019. The stories are printed by the permission of the author.

The stories 'Arrival', 'Psyche', 'Mr Storage', and 'Epic of the New Colony' were first published in *Shab Khoon*, Allahabad. 'A Half-Serious Story' was first published in *Jawaz*, Malegaon. All the stories are taken from *Nai Basti Ka Razmia Aur Digar Afsane* by Mahmoud Yasien, Mizgan Publications, Kolkata, 2015. The stories are printed by the permission of the author.

The story 'The Shop of Words' is taken from *Urdu Ki Khwateen Fiction Nigar*, Sahitya Akademi, New Delhi, 2014. The story is printed by the permission of the author.

The story 'Similar' is taken from *Parinde* (*Afsanvi Majmua*) by Anisun Nabi, published by Anisun Nabi, New Delhi, 2012. The story is printed by the permission of the author.

The stories 'The Watch' and 'When Peace Came Around' are taken from *Jo Ama'a Mili* (short stories) by Reyaz Danish, Danish Publication, Kolkata, 2019. The stories are printed by the permission of the author.

ABOUT THE AUTHORS

Sayeed Premi was born in 1937 and passed away in 2015 in Kolkata. He did his Masters in History from the University of Calcutta and taught History at the Islamia High School from where he retired in 1997. He was the Ward Councillor for five years and also the Mayor-in-Council for a brief period. He has two collections of stories and also a novelette.

Firoz Abid (pen name of Md. Firozuddin) was born in 1943 in Kolkata. He has done his Masters in Urdu from the University of Calcutta. He was a school teacher at a government school and retired as the Headmaster of Woodburn School in Calcutta. His literary works include three collections of short stories, *Andhi Gali Mein Subah, Naqsh Bar Aab*, and *Khule Aasman Ke Niche*. He has received numerous awards like a National Award in 1991 and the Imtiyaz-e-Meer Award, 1997, from Meer Academy, Lucknow. Most of his stories have been published in *Shab Khoon*, Allahabad. His poems have been published in various Urdu magazines. He has translated many

Bengali short stories into Urdu and has written innumerable textbooks for school children. He spends his retired life with his family in Kolkata.

Anis Rafi (pen name of Anisur Rahman Khan) was born in Vaishali, Bihar in 1945. He completed his schooling and higher education in Calcutta. He worked for 14 years at All India Radio and at Doordarshan for 16 years. He also taught at Aligarh Muslim University, as well as Calcutta. He has written more than a hundred stories. He has won numerous awards, including the West Bengal Urdu Academy and the U.P. Urdu Academy awards. He has three collections of published short stories, *Ab Woh Utarney Wala Hai, Curfew Sakht Hai*, and *Gadagar Sarai*. His stories have been translated into Hindi, Bengali, Punjabi, Assamese, and English. After retirement, he has made Kolkata his permanent home.

Siddique Alam, novelist, short story writer, playwright, poet, and critic was born in 1952 in Purulia, West Bengal. His three novels, four collections of short stories, and a collection of poems have been published in India. He has also published two novels, two collections of short stories and a translation of J.M. Coetzee's *Waiting for the Barbarians* from Pakistan. The American literary website: https://www.wordswithoutborders.org/ included him in its issue dedicated to Urdu Fiction of India.

The University of Wisconsin-Madison published his short stories for three consecutive years (2010–2012) in its *Annual of Urdu Studies.* He has been included in anthologies like *River of Flesh* compiled by Ruchira Gupta from 13 languages, and *The Greatest Urdu Short Stories Ever Told* by Muhammad Umar Memon. His works have also been included in other anthologies and his stories have been translated into different languages. He retired from Government service in 2012 and has settled in Kolkata.

Mahmoud Yasien (pen name of Mahmood Alam) was born in 1954 in Kolkata. He taught at a school for 10 years. His first story was published in *Tej Weekly*. Later, literary figures like Shamsur Rahman Farooqi and Baqar Mehdi published his stories in *Shab Khoon*, Allahabad, and *Izhaar*, Bombay. Many of his stories have been published in magazines like *Shair*, *Jawaz*, and *Shama*. He has translated English stories of writers such as Graham Greene, Edgar Allan Poe, and the French writer Alain Robbe-Grillet. He has two volumes of short stories published from Kolkata. He lives with his wife in Kolkata.

Shahira Masroor was born in Kolkata in 1958 and educated in the city. She did her Masters in Urdu literature. She wrote stories from an early age. Her first story *Safar Se Wapsi* was published in *Shair*. Later, her stories were also published in magazines such as *Shab Khoon, Jawaz, Aaj Kal, Ruh-e-Adab,* and *Suhail.* Her collection of short stories *Safar Se Wapsi* was published in 1990. She leads a quiet life in Kolkata.

Anisun Nabi (pen name of Syed Anisun Nabi) was born in 1958 in Kolkata. He did his Masters in Urdu from the University of Calcutta. His literary work consists of plays, and a collection of short stories *Parinde* (2013) which won the West Bengal Urdu Academy award and the Sahir Ludhyanvi and Dilip Kumar Award (2013) by Fankar Academy. His plays like *Hangama Hai Kyun Barpa*, and *Kahan Lagaun Bistar* are popular. He has also written tele-films for Bollywood like *Agent* 007 (1990) and *Shaitani Raat* (1991). He was a dialogue writer of feature films like *Darawani Haveli* (1997) and *Bombay Crime* (2003). He was a regular column writer in *Aabshaar*, Calcutta, for three years, as well as in a monthly *Jhalak*. His profession is numerology. He lives with his family in Kolkata.

Reyaz Danish (pen name of Reyaz Ahmed) was born in 1969 in Kolkata. He is a teacher who developed a love for writing short stories early in life. His first story was published in *Rooh-e-Adab* in 2006. His first collection *Jo Ama'a Mili* was published in 2019. He lives with his family in Kolkata.